HAPPY HOWL-O-WEEN HORROR

COUNTRY COTTAGE MYSTERIES 20

ADDISON MOORE

BELLAMY BLOOM

BOOK DESCRIPTION

The Country Cottage Inn is known for its hospitality. Leaving can be murder.

My name is Bizzy Baker, and I can read minds. Not every mind, not every *time*, but most of the time, and believe me when I say, it's not all it's cracked up to be.

It's October in Cider Cove, and Mayor Woods has decided to change the name of our cozy little town to *Spider* Cove for the entire month. But when a body turns up at the zombie walk, things take a turn for the deadly. Add in an ex-boyfriend of mine who is making Jasper insane with jealousy, along with an eerie cult obsessed with werewolves, and you have a hairy, scary month of terror ahead. Halloween is upon us, and I don't know if Cider Cove will ever be the same again.

Bizzy Baker runs the Country Cottage Inn, has the ability to pry into the darkest recesses of both the human and animal mind, and has just stumbled upon a body. With the help of her kitten, *Fish*, a mutt named Sherlock Bones, and an ornery yet dangerously good-looking homicide detective, Bizzy is determined to find the killer.

Cider Cove, Maine is the premier destination for fun and relaxation. But when a body turns up, it's the premier destination for murder.

CHAPTER 1

"*Boo!*" a pale-faced, bruised eye, missing teeth, scraggly-haired zombie shouts as congealed blood oozes down the side of his face.

A scream evicts from me as I jump back, just in time to have candy corn rain down over me.

"We got you, Bizzy!" a wild cackle comes from my right, and I turn to find Georgie Conner laughing and slapping her thigh. She's holding a bucket full of the seasonal confection and is dressed like a zombie herself. Georgie is an eighty-something hippie with a shock of gray wiry hair and a hardcore love of both kaftans and testing my sanity. "We got you good! And now we're going to eat your *brain!*"

Fish, my sweet black and white tabby, hisses at the two zombies in front of us. *We'll get them good, Bizzy.* She takes a moment to lash her tail at the red and white freckled mutt at my feet. *Come on, you big oaf. Bite their rotting heads off. We need to protect Bizzy before they eat her brain. Lord knows, Jasper has already started in on it.*

I pause as I frown down at the feisty feline in my arms. Fish has been with me now for going on three years, and we're closer than sisters.

Sherlock Bones, the aforementioned red and white freckled oaf, or mutt as it were, gives a sharp bark at the monsters before us as they laugh their rotten heads off. *You better run the other way, weirdos, or I'll be forced to show you what I'm made of.*

Oh, good grief, Fish moans. *Now is not the time to show off your bacon prowess. These creatures might prefer bacon to brains.*

It's true—not the part about bacon to brains, but the fact that Sherlock Bones is mostly made of the salted meat by now. Not a shocker, considering he consumes his weight in bacon every chance he gets.

Sherlock Bones came into my life exactly two years ago—at the same time my husband stepped onto the scene. Jasper and I have been married for one year, and life has been bliss—with the exception of the steady string of homicides that seems to be taking place, but I choose not to think about that at the moment.

It's October in Cider Cove, and Mayor Woods, my shiny

new sister-in-law, has decided to rename our sweet coastal town to something that the tourists might want to flock to at this spooky time of year. For the entire month of October, Cider Cove will officially be known as *Spider* Cove. And to kick off this haunted month in style, every soul in town is congregating right here on Main Street for the Spider Cove Halloween Spooktacular.

Young and old alike have donned costumes for the occasion, as have the furry among us. Each shop is decorated to the hilt with maple leaves, corn husks, scarecrows, and pumpkins of every shape and size. There are witches, ghosts, and goblins—as well as the obligatory spiders in every shape and size festooning the shop windows—and the real deals happen to be roaming the cobbled streets this evening as well.

An autumn breeze picks up as the chill in the air intensifies. The scent of fried apple fritters and hot apple cider tickles our senses as a plethora of food vendors have taken their wares to the streets to entice the crowds that have shown up for this evening's horror fest.

Georgie pulls the zombie next to her close. "All right, hot stuff. It's time you met the scariest person in all of Spider Cove, Bizzy Baker Wilder. The alien cat in her arms is Fish. And the half-shark, half-pooch is Sherlock Bones."

Sherlock barks. *I told you they'd know what I was!* He jumps with glee at the thought and his tail wags like a pendulum.

Both Fish and Sherlock loathe dressing up for any occasion, let alone Halloween. So when I suggested they dress up for the entire month of October, they predictably threatened to stage a revolt. But when I told them I'd let them choose their own costumes, they reconsidered. I let them pick several to wear throughout the month and, dare I say, they're actually looking forward to donning them all. Tonight, Fish has a silver UFO cinched around her waist—think tutu—and a green hood over her head with giant dark eyes and a tiny mouth sewn over it to complete her alien appeal.

Sherlock simply has a large gray fin over his back. Even though he's agreed to play dress-up for the month, he made sure his contribution to the effort was kept at a bare minimum.

I've donned a headband with a pair of cat ears attached and called it a day. Suffice it to say, I should probably step up my costume game, too.

"Bizzy"—Georgie slings an arm over the shoulder of the hellion standing next to her—"this is my buddy, Billy the Butcher. He's my partner in brain-eating crime for the zombie walk." She glances over at him. "You better watch it, Billy. Bizzy's a butcher in her own right. She's going on two dozen homicides now, and her killing streak is hotter than ever."

The man with the face of death, dark hair sticking straight up, and clothes in tatters, laughs. He's wearing a dull green jacket over his holey shirt and rag-like jeans. Across the jacket's right arm are two yellow stripes in a wide V, conjoined, like a couple of spooning arrows.

"I keep telling her my name isn't Billy." He tosses his hand my way, and it happens to be covered with the same pale gray makeup that's caked over his face and neck. "Barnabas Casper. My friends call me Barnabas." He pretends to shoot me when he says it. *Geez, she's cute. Black hair and blue eyes are my favorite combo. And that body? I might be playing the part of the walking dead, but I'd show her exactly how alive I could be if I could land her in my bedroom. I bet I can make every last delicious inch of her feel just as alive, if not more.* His thoughts dissipate as something akin to white noise takes over.

My name is Bizzy Baker Wilder, and I can read minds— not every mind, not every time—but it happens, and believe me, it's not all it's cracked up to be. Yes, I can read the animal mind as well, and sometimes they have better things to say than most humans. And I'm not sure how, but the animals always seem to understand each other. I'm glad about it, too.

Fish mewls up at me, *He's taken his thoughts elsewhere, hasn't he, Bizzy?*

I frown and nod at the very same time, without bothering to take my eyes off the monster before me. I try not to judge people for their thoughts—especially since they have no idea I'm prying into them—but knowing that Barnabas here is doing who knows what with yours truly isn't exactly what I would call thrilling.

"Nice to meet you, Barnabas," I growl his way.

Sherlock barks. *You're not telling the truth, Bizzy. I can tell because your lips are twitching. Your lips always twitch when you wish you could say something you really mean.*

If I said what I really meant, I might actually frighten the man far more than any monster on Main Street at the moment could hope to do.

Georgie hops and slings her arm over my shoulder instead. "Bizzy owns the Country Cottage Inn just down the street. She not only knows how to bring home the bacon, but she can fry it up in a pan."

No, she can't! Sherlock barks once again. *And now Georgie's lying, too. Does not telling the truth have something to do with Halloween? Because if it does, I think I should be warned. If someone offers me a strip of bacon, and I get a flavorless doggie biscuit instead, I'll be spittin' mad.*

5

Fish moans. *It's an expression, you goof. Bizzy is an astute businesswoman. Bacon stands for money. Everyone knows Bizzy can't cook worth a lick. Even this brain-eater that Georgie dragged over can probably sense it. Bizzy would burn down all of Cider Cove if she tried to fry up some bacon. Excuse me,* **Spider** *Cove.*

I'm right back to frowning again.

She's not wrong. The fact Baker is my surname is something akin to a cosmic joke.

"The inn down the street?" Barnabas is suddenly jolted out of his white-noise stupor. "That place is huge. I parked in the overflow lot to come up here. I run a software company. If you'd like, I'll do a free consult—check under the hood and see how your computers are doing."

Fish snorts. *I bet he'd like to check under your hood.*

Sherlock growls, *Jasper better get back quickly. Or I might just arrange for this dearly departed clown to dearly depart.*

I'm about to say something when a loud bullhorn goes off and all eyes are redirected toward the gazebo at the end of the street. The tall, white structure is decorated with enough artificial spider webs to encircle the Earth twice, and on the roof of the gazebo sits a black, hairy spider with red glowing eyes. If anyone suffers from arachnophobia, I'd suggest they skip popping into our cozy little town for the next thirty-one days, and maybe a week after that. This monstrous mess is going to take more than a few days to clean up.

Mayor Woods—Mackenzie Woods, the woman who married my brother last February and just gave birth to his son less than two weeks ago—steps up to the podium set in the gazebo. She's a tall brunette dressed in a navy power suit. I'm not sure how she's done it, but she's squeezed back into her old clothes in record time.

Mackenzie's belly was the size of a beach ball just prior to landing a seven-pound bouncing baby boy into my brother's arms. But she looks more or less like her old self now.

My brother Huxley is an attorney who is taking a couple of months off for paternity leave. Mackenzie isn't exactly what you would call maternal, but that's not really a surprise to any of us. True to her word, less than two days after pushing out baby Mack—yes, she named the baby after herself—she went straight to her office and began to do whatever it is that keeps her busy from nine to five. Huxley and my mother have been taking care of the baby in the interim—and quite possibly beyond.

"Attention, one and all!" Mackenzie shouts into the microphone. "Welcome to Spider Cove, where it's Halloween every day in October!"

The crowd goes wild.

There's an even split between the young and old. The younger kids look adorable with their colorful costumes and happy plastic pumpkins already brimming with treats. The teenagers among us look a bit gruesome. Most everyone has brought their pets along, and they're happily, or unhappily, dressed for spooktacular success as well.

Mackenzie raises a hand. "Spider Cove will be hosting special events all month long, like the pumpkin carving contest, the preschool processional, the Howl-o-ween parade of pets, and we'll finish off with zombies once again on the unholy night itself, followed by live music and dancing! And tonight we're kicking off this spooktacular night with a good old-fashioned zombie walk." The crowd whoops with approval at the thought of being overrun with an entire herd of undead, hungry for gray matter. "But first is the unveiling of what will be the centerpiece of Spider Cove for the duration of this haunted month." She waves a hand to the park on her left where a large object sits at least twenty feet high with a large white tarp draped over it. "On three!" She counts backward, and the crowd counts right along with her. When she gets to one, the tarp is yanked off and every soul in Spider Cove gasps at the adorable sight.

A giant smiling jack-o'-lantern stands as proud and orange as it can be, with a tiny cap of green leaves circling around its stem. I'm not sure if it's plastic, resin, or wood, but that thing is massive, and already people are jockeying to take pictures with it. Believe me, I plan to do the same.

"Thank you for coming out tonight," she continues. "Please enjoy the rest of the festivities. The food vendors are all local, and the *free* spider web cupcakes have been generously donated by the Country Cottage Inn." She takes a moment to snark my way. Mackenzie and I were once the best of friends, but that ended eons ago in high school. We more or less tolerate one another now. But I appreciate the fact she's highlighting the inn. "And don't forget to patronize the shops right here in Spider Cove," Mackenzie shouts before stepping down from the podium.

Spooky music seeps through unseen speakers as the crowd grows wild once again.

I wave over at my best friend Emmie, who is working the dessert table in front of the gazebo, passing out spider web cupcakes to the masses. I knew they'd be a hit—chocolate with white vanilla frosting and a black web pattern on top. Who could resist that? Plus, the fact that Emmie has been churning them out—that alone guarantees they'll be delicious.

Emmie isn't only my best friend, she runs the Country Cottage Café that's attached to the inn. Emmie and I share the same long black hair and baby blue eyes. We also share the same formal moniker of *Elizabeth*, but neither of us has ever gone by it.

"Back to my offer." Barnabas nods my way with those dark, bruised eyes. A professional makeup artist offered up her services for tonight's haunted endeavor, and everyone who volunteered for the zombie walk looks fresh from the graveyard. "You say when and where, and I'll be there." *Here's hoping her bed fits the bill for the latter.*

A dull laugh lives and dies in my chest.

Dream on, zombie boy.

A tall man with dark curly hair, coffee-colored eyes, and a polished-looking suit comes up and hooks his arm around Barnabas' neck, pretending to give him a noogie.

"Is this deadhead bothering you?" He sheds an easy grin my way, and we both gasp at the very same time. "Bizzy Baker?"

"Griffin Duncan?" My jaw roots to the ground as I take him in.

Before we can process what's panning out to be a blast from the past, Mackenzie trots over as fast as her kitten heels will allow.

"Griffin Duncan!" She throws her arms around him, and he laughs as they partake in a hearty embrace. "I can't believe it's you. And wow, you're still as hot as ever."

He gives a sheepish grin, but it's true for the most part. Griffin is still a looker.

A tall, dark, and handsome man holding two candy apples rolled in peanuts, chocolate chips, and cookie crumbles strolls up onto the scene.

"What's going on?" Jasper asks as he nods to the man who can't seem to take his eyes off of me.

"Griffin"—I clear my throat—"I'd love for you to meet my

husband, Jasper Wilder." I glance to my handsome hubby. "Jasper, this is Griffin Duncan. We went to high school together."

Griffin chuckles as he nods to Jasper. "Bizzy and I were homecoming king and queen, senior year. We dated hot and heavy."

Hot and heavy? Fish mewls, but it sounds more like a devious giggle. *Oh, this is going to be good.*

Sherlock barks. *No, it's not. No wonder he's drooling your way as if you were a juicy steak. He wants to eat Jasper's dinner!*

I'm not even going to touch that.

"Hot and heavy?" Jasper rocks back on his heels, his expression darkening a notch—and if I didn't know better, I think his elbow just touched the butt of his gun.

"That's right," Mackenzie says as she wraps her arms around Griffin's waist. "But then Griffy came to his senses and started dating me."

More like she swiped him from under me, the same way she swiped every other boyfriend I had—thus the reason our friendship hit the skids.

Griffin, by the way, was the last straw as far as my friendship with Mackenzie was concerned—or I guess you could say *last* boyfriend. Mack says she was simply doing me a favor by seeing which boys would be loyal to me—and it turns out, the answer was none. But I wasn't too appreciative of her efforts back then.

"I'm in town again," Griffin says with his eyes still hypnotically hooked to mine. "I'm staying right here at the little inn for a bit. I can't wait to catch up with you."

Georgie cackles like a witch in training. "At the little inn?

Why, Bizzy owns the little inn, and she happens to live there, too."

"Well then…" Barnabas, the zombie, says just as a redheaded golden retriever runs up. His coat glows the color of a pumpkin, and on his head sits an orange pointed hat wrapped in twinkle lights. "It looks as if I've got two reasons to visit the Country Cottage Inn." He scoops up the adorable puppy, and it licks a line of that gray pancake makeup right off the side of his face.

Griffin shakes his head while looking right at me. "Sorry, Barn, my schedule is all booked up." His smile widens as he takes me in. "After all, this king has to get reacquainted with his queen."

Mackenzie growls.

Georgie howls.

And Jasper looks as if he's about to commit murder.

A crisp breeze rustles by and a chill runs up my spine at the thought.

Something tells me there's a homicide on the horizon, all right. And I pray Jasper Wilder won't be responsible for it.

CHAPTER 2

*T*he Spider Cove Halloween Spooktacular is in full effect with bodies large and small mobbing Main Street. The air is crisp, and the candy apple Jasper just handed me is even crisper.

"So what do you do for a living?" Griffin asks Jasper with a quasi-disgruntled look on his face.

The fact Griffin insisted on sharing a few key details about our flash in the pan relationship isn't sitting well with Jasper, I can tell.

King and queen of homecoming? Old news.

And the fact we were hot and heavy? Maybe it was true, but for all of two weeks. I hardly call that a history. But he was memorable, I'll give him that.

Thoughts of those steamy kisses we shared flood my mind, and for once I'm more than thankful Jasper can't read my thoughts. But despite that fact, I quickly banish any more of the lip-lock visuals.

I'm a firm believer in the fact that the past has no place in the present—especially in the present where I'm exceedingly happy with my husband. And I'd like to keep it that way.

"I'm a homicide detective down in Seaview," Jasper grumbles, the apple in his hand untouched. I'm guessing he's lost his appetite. He extends the apple toward Georgie, as if he read my mind indeed, and she takes the red globe from him with glee.

"A homicide detective?" Griffin looks taken aback. "That's impressive. I guess I don't associate the state of Maine with too many of those. I can't imagine the homicide rate is all that high."

"You'd be surprised," Jasper says the words sharp and it sounded like a threat.

Barnabas chuckles. "I get a death threat once a week." He winks over at Georgie and she scoffs.

"Tell me about it, hot stuff." She points his way with the apple in her hand. "People are always disparaging our kind. Little do they know we can't get any deader than this."

Barnabas howls with laughter. "It looks as if I got paired up with the right ghoul. Ain't we just dead and dandy."

"Dead and dandy!" Georgie hoots and hollers and drops the candy apple right out of her hand.

Both Sherlock and the redheaded golden retriever make a play for it, but Georgie catches it midair and smashes it over her bedraggled-looking kaftan where it leaves a sticky red splotch.

"Eh." She shrugs. "It looks like blood."

The golden retriever gives a few yips as it struggles to lunge forward and wrap its mouth around the treat.

"Oh no, you don't," Barnabas says as he attaches a leash to the dog and sets it down. "The last thing you need is an upset tummy."

"Aw," I coo as I give the little cutie a quick pat. "What's its name?"

"Her name is Nutmeg," Barnabas says as he gives her a pat himself. "She's six months old—all puppy. All she wants to do is play."

"You came to the right place, kiddo," Georgie says, taking the leash for him. "How about we burn some of this puppy energy off with bacon?"

Sherlock barks and jumps. *I'm a puppy, too, Georgie!*

Fish scoffs. *He would admit to being a giraffe if that's what it took to land a piece of salted meat in his mouth.*

It's true, but in his defense, a lot of people would admit to being a giraffe if bacon was on the line.

Both dogs go nuts as Georgie lets the bacon fly, and Barnabas laughs.

"All right, you little devil," Barnabas says, pulling Nutmeg back a notch. "I'd better walk this pooch if I expect her to behave the rest of the night." He looks my way a moment. *I'd tell her I meant what I said about checking her systems, but now that I know her husband is packing heat, I think I'll retreat. Besides, it looks as if Griffin isn't going to let a little holy matrimony get in his way. Not surprising. The guy thinks he's above the law.* He nods to Georgie as he starts to walk off. "I'll be back in time for our walk, cutie."

"You better be," she shouts after him. "Nobody does dead better than you." She looks up at Griffin. "How about you, good-looking? Are you into dead chicks?" She staggers his way, and he laughs.

"As tempting as the offer is, I happen to like my women very much alive." He winks my way, and I can feel Jasper stiffen by my side.

Mackenzie smirks before caressing Griffin's cheek and turning his head until he lands his full attention on her.

"You always did like a girl who could get your heart pumping," she purrs.

Jasper and I exchange a glance.

Is she flirting with him? Jasper asks while shaking his head as if trying to deny the obvious.

And as tempted as I am to answer him, I bite my tongue.

"Mackenzie just had a baby," I say to Griffin. "Doesn't she look great?"

Mackenzie snarls my way, and I bite back a smile threatening to unleash.

She's got to be kidding me. What's there to snarl about? She's married—to my brother.

"A baby?" Griffin inches back as he inspects her. "Congratulations. You look fantastic." He swings his gaze my way. "And you look *incredible*, Bizzy."

Mackenzie is right back to snarling. *Leave it to Bizzy to try to make me sound like a matronly hausfrau. I didn't let her steal the limelight when we were kids, and I won't let her steal it now.*

I can't help it. I'm practically programmed to steal her boyfriends.

She's not wrong.

Jasper nods to Griffin. "So what do you do?"

Griffin rocks back on his heels and grimaces. "I'm recently divorced." A smile tugs at his lips as he looks my way as if that uncalled-for relationship tidbit was meant to entice me. His smile dissipates as he looks over at Jasper. "My ex and I opened a bar and grill, Lucky Thirteen, out in Edison. And since my ex and I are still good friends, we've decided to keep it up and running rather than buy one another out or shut the doors." His chest broadens as he looks my way.

"You're being modest." Mackenzie playfully swats him. "Tell them about Drive. Everyone knows that's your baby."

"Drive?" Jasper asks. "As in the rideshare company?"

"Drive? *Ohh*, baby." Georgie rubs her hands together. "You must be rolling in it."

"I'm swimming in it." He flashes that smile my way again.

"That's right," Mackenzie says as she links her arm through his. "Griffin Duncan is the most successful businessman that graduated from our class."

A dull laugh huffs from Jasper. "I don't know, I bet Bizzy could give him a run for his money."

"Is that so?" Griffin lifts a brow. "We'll have to get together and exchange financials. Consider it a date."

Both Jasper and Sherlock growl.

Fish mewls in amusement, *There's going to be a dog fight soon, Bizzy. With Jasper starting the party.*

I don't think she's that far off the mark.

Griffin's face brightens as he looks past me and gives a friendly wave at someone over my shoulder.

I turn that way to see a redhead in a red and black buffalo plaid jacket heading this way.

"Griffin Duncan?" She shakes her head with a laugh. "I knew I'd be meeting up with a few shady characters here today, but I didn't think you'd be one of them."

"Everyone, this is my good friend, Sabrina Chambers," he says as he chuckles her way. "Sabrina works for the Montgomerys' farm. My ex is big on buying local for Lucky Thirteen, and Sabrina is our point person."

The redhead lifts her brows. "And I always make sure you get choice produce." Her attention is snagged by something over by the gazebo. "Well, if it isn't…" she says that last bit mostly to herself.

I glance that way and spot Barnabas standing in front of the dessert table where Emmie is handing out the spider web cupcakes at breakneck pace. There's a surly-looking man with dark scraggly hair and facial scruff to match who seems to be having a heated conversation with the zombie in question. Honestly, the only reason I know it's Barnabas is due to the fact he's got Nutmeg with him. Apart from the perky pooch, he looks indistinguishable from the rest of the zombies staggering in the vicinity.

"Excuse me." Sabrina's nostrils flare as she looks that way. *That SOB mocks me at every turn. I can't believe he's wearing it. And masquerading as the dead? He deserves to be dead, all right.* "I have a sudden hankering for a little dessert."

"I think I'll join you," Griffin says. "I've got a sweet tooth blooming myself." He glances my way. *And Bizzy Baker is the exact sweet treat I'm craving.*

Wonderful. I frown up at him without meaning to.

"Allow me," Mackenzie says. "I'll give you both the grand tour of the dessert table. We have over seven of Cider Cove's

17

—pardon me, *Spider* Cove's, best eateries contributing to the kickoff festival." She quickly whisks them both in the direction of the dessert table, and by the time they get there, the scruffy man has disappeared and Sabrina seems to have cornered Barnabas herself. She gives him a shove, then does her best to yank off his jacket.

"Oh wow," I moan as I watch in horror. "I think that woman, Sabrina, is attacking the man with the dog."

Georgie grunts as she squints that way, "Nah, she's just trying to undress him. It's the curse of our kind. Humans find us irresistible." She nods to Jasper. "Word to the wise: get yourself in a zombie getup and you might get lucky. My makeup artist is around here somewhere, and she's a real gem."

Please,* Fish huffs. *If only Georgie knew how little Jasper had to do to get lucky, as she puts it. The man blinks and he's lucky.

I waggle my brows at Jasper. She's right, of course. But who could blame me?

He lifts his chin. "Is that your way of telling me I need to find a makeup artist before setting foot in the bedroom?"

"I would never send you in the direction of another woman," I tell him.

"Nor would I go. I've already got the perfect woman who can do it all."

Sherlock barks. ***She can't cook.***

Both Fish and I give Sherlock the stink eye.

Jasper leans in. "Why do I get the feeling Sherlock is in the doghouse?"

A chipper blonde pops up. "That's because my sister is a beast."

My sister Macy laughs as she slings an arm around my shoulders.

Macy is older than me by a year and is my polar opposite in just about every way. She's a self-proclaimed maneater, always on the prowl for her next snack. She owns a soap and candle shop right here on Main Street. In fact, that's where I found Fish when she was a kitten—in the alley behind Lather and Light.

Macy's white fuzzy Samoyed trots up by her side, dressed in a hot pink tutu with dozens of long-stranded pearls looped around her neck.

"Hey, Candy," I say, ignoring my sister momentarily in lieu of greeting her pooch. "You look adorable. What are you supposed to be?"

"She's a socialite," Macy answers for her. "And so am I, in the event you were wondering." She fingers the pearls looped around her own neck. Other than the pearls, Macy is wearing a cranberry suit made of crepe fabric and matching three-inch heels—her usual go-to attire when working at her shop. Macy is essentially a socialite without all the gobs of money to go along with the job title.

"Clever," I say. I'm about to ask if she's making it mandatory for her employees to dress up for the month when the sound of chanting stops me cold.

The voices of a large group of women shouting something at top volume only seem to grow with intensity, but for the life of me I can't make out what they're saying.

"What is that about?" I ask as I crane my neck past the gazebo where the voices seem to be emanating from.

"It's that time of year," Georgie says. "The women are out for blood."

"What kind of blood?" Jasper asks with a stern edge to his voice. I can tell that entire episode with Griffin has him on a homicidal edge.

19

"Blood of the male variety," Georgie points out.

Macy shakes my shoulder. "Look, there they are." She points down the street, and sure enough, a group of chanting women heads for the woods just past town square, and each one of them is wearing a crimson hooded robe like the kind you'd see on a monk, long and relatively creepy.

One of the women breaks from the group as she pulls off her hood and heads for the dessert table.

"Hey, I think I know her," Macy marvels. "I think that's Carrie Hazelman. She's one of my best customers. She practically buys by the pallet. She's got like six homes she likes to keep stocked with my goods."

"Wow, she must be loaded," I muse. "You charge a fortune."

Jasper ticks his head. "In other words, she's paying your rent."

"You got that right," Macy says. "It's practically my duty to go over and break cupcakes with her. While I'm at it, I'll find out what the deal with the red robe society is." She pats me on the back. "See there, Bizzy? You're not the only amateur sleuth in the family." She starts to take off, then backtracks. "Ooh, I almost forgot. She's allergic to dogs." She hands Candy's leash over to me. "I'll be back."

She takes off and Candy barks after her. *Bring me a cupcake, please.*

She won't do it. Sherlock barks softly at the white furball. *I already tried to talk Bizzy into snagging a spider web cupcake for me. But she says they're deadly to dogs.*

Fish sits up in my arms. *I think I'll head to the dessert table and snag myself a few of those pest removers. Exactly how many would you say it would take to be lethal?* She extends her claws as she looks my way.

"Haha, I'm not laughing." I give her nose a tap.

"Look at that." Jasper nods toward the dessert table and we see that woman in the red robe shoving what looks to be a cupcake into Barnabas' mouth—and not in any friendly manner.

Speaking of cupcakes, Griffin and that redhead from the Montgomerys' farm each look to be enjoying one of the sweet treats themselves. In fact, Barnabas has one in each hand and one in his mouth at the moment.

The sound of a bullhorn goes off—three short toots—and soon Mackenzie is back at the podium announcing that it's time for the zombie walk.

As soon as all of the major players—dead players to be exact—are in place, the processional starts from the gazebo as an entire herd of the undead lurch and sway their way down the middle of the cobbled street.

Georgie staggers over with Barnabas hanging onto her shoulders from behind. She's grunting and groaning as Barnabas lies slumped over her back.

She comes in close and Fish jumps right out of my arms. I can't blame her, Georgie makes a darn good zombie.

I laugh as I step forward. "You guys are doing great."

"Yeah, I'm on fire," Georgie moans. "But this kid is turning out to be a real drag. He's been nothing but dead weight." She sloughs him off with a shake of the shoulders and Barnabas lunges in my direction, but I don't dare move. I've never been one to lose a game of chicken.

Barnabas doesn't waver either. Instead, he lands on top of me and we both go down to the ground like a couple of dominos.

"Whoa," I say as Jasper quickly comes to our aid. "You're right, Georgie," I tease. "This guy really is dead weight."

"Geez, are you okay, Bizzy?" Jasper asks as he helps me to my feet.

"I'm fine." I laugh it up as I dust myself off.

"Not funny, buddy," Jasper says as he tries to help Barnabas up as well. "All right, have it your way. Play dead all you want."

Foam seeps from Barnabas' mouth and I inch back. His eyes are opened and unblinking, his chest unmoving.

"Check his vitals," I pant.

"What?" Jasper shakes his head. "I'm not falling for it."

"Just do it," I insist.

This entire night is getting to me. As soon as Jasper says he's fine, we're heading home.

Jasper checks the man's pulse at the wrist, then at his jugular, too, before looking up at me and shaking his head.

"He's gone." Jasper sighs as he says it.

Barnabas won't be looking under anyone's hood ever again.

Barnabas Casper is dead.

CHAPTER 3

"*H*e's dead," Jasper says as he pulls out his phone and calls for assistance.

Another zombie staggers into our midst. "He's dead?" Her bruised eyes widen as she takes him in and lets out a blood-curdling scream. Soon, a small crowd of zombies breaks out in a similar cry before strutting away moaning for brains.

Fish yodels along with them, as does Sherlock.

"Those people think we're kidding," I say, horrified.

23

Georgie grunts, "They think *he's* kidding." She gives Barnabas a swift kick to the ribs.

"*Georgie,*" I call out, aghast.

"What?" she says, snatching Fish from me. "That's how we used to check for corpses when we were kids—we'd kick 'em."

Fish yowls, *Let's kick him and run, Bizzy. This month was going to be stressful enough without having a body to tend to.*

You mean an investigation. Sherlock barks. *I don't say this often, Fish, but you're right. I say we leave this investigation in Jasper's capable hands.*

Fish brays out a laugh and sounds like a dolphin chortling her way through the ocean blue.

The Spider Cove Halloween Spooktacular rages all around us as creepy music seeps from the speakers and zombies strut their staccato stuff as a parade of those undead menaces takes over all of Main Street. The scent of fresh grilled hot dogs ignites my senses as darkness settles over our tiny seaside town.

"We don't know if there's been a homicide," I say to the furry among us, and Jasper gives me a look that says *you've got to be kidding.*

"You're right." I close my eyes a moment. "The poor man fell on me. I'm practically the Grim Reaper at this point."

Macy clip-clops up along with the redheaded golden retriever puppy, Nutmeg.

Georgie nudges my sister as she nods my way. "Someone here never went corpse kicking as a child and it shows."

Macy glances at me. "Maybe, but she's making up for lost time. Try not to kill anyone today, would you?" She turns back to Georgie. "Where's your dead partner in crime? I just spoke to Carrie Hazelman. The man is worth billions."

A group of kids walks by, no taller than my knee, and a

few of them dig into their plastic pumpkins and toss a handful of candy at poor Barnabas as he lies on the ground. The one dressed as Batman kicks him in the shin before his mother yanks him away.

"*Billions?*" Jasper and I say in unison.

"Look at you two." Georgie shakes her head. "A man is dead and all you can think about is money."

Nutmeg runs over to Barnabas as the twinkle lights on her hat blink on and off. *Get up*, she yowls at him. *You've got a parade to tend to. And then you promised me a burger, remember? This isn't the time for a nap.* She turns to Sherlock. *Although, my human has been known to out nap me almost every day of the week. He's always telling me that adulting is hard.*

Fish mewls down at the redheaded cutie, *Oh dear, I'm sorry, Nutmeg. But I don't think your human will be waking up from this nap.*

What? Nutmeg cocks her head as if she's not computing. Death rarely does for so many of us.

It's true. Sherlock nuzzles his head against her tiny neck. It's okay, kid. *Fish and I will stay with you until we can figure things out. You'll be safe and cared for. And I'll even give you all my bacon just to make you feel better.*

Candy struts up. *I'll be here for you, too. The same thing happened to my human. But I'm with Macy now, and I'm safe and loved. And, I promise, you'll be safe and loved, too.*

Nutmeg starts in on a howl, and you can feel the grief in her voice. Fish jumps out of Georgie's arms, and both Candy and Sherlock surround Nutmeg as they try their best to comfort her.

"Jasper," a deep voice calls out from the crowd as Deputy Leo Granger, Jasper's best friend who happens to be married to my best friend, jogs over in his tan deputy uniform. "What the hell is going on?"

Jasper quickly fills him in, and soon they're creating a barricade around the body. Leo happens to share my mind-reading quirk. He's the one that told me that we're both something called transmundane, further classified as telesensual. Apparently, there are a myriad of supernatural abilities that fall under the transmundane umbrella, and mind reading happens to be one of them.

I pull Macy and Georgie to the side just as my mother runs up.

Ree Baker is petite, sharp as a tack, and has an everlasting devotion to all things eighties. Her caramel blonde hair is coiffed and feathered as an ode to that neon decade, and she's wearing corduroys and a green poplin blouse with the collar lifted around her ears. Her face is painted to resemble a Day of the Dead skeleton—paper-white with blue dots to create an outline around her features, pink hearts over her cheeks, and her lips are colored in a dark shade of crimson. Mom isn't one to play dress-up, so the fact she's gone as far as painting her face lets me know she's jumping into the Halloween spirit with both skeletal feet.

"What is going on, young lady?" Mom gives my elbow a yank. "I saw that man fall over you. My goodness, Bizzy, you're not a serial killer, are you?"

"Mother," I snip as I yank my elbow back. "You, of all people, should know the answer to that."

She makes a face. *Believe me, at this point I'd rather not answer.*

I gasp at the thought.

"Don't worry, kiddo." Georgie pats me on the arm. "We'll cover for you."

Macy nods. "And I'll sleep with any cop that tries to arrest you."

The three of us gape at her.

"What?" She presses a hand to her chest. "I'm taking one for the team. You'd do the same for me, Bizzy."

"Hardly," Mom balks. "But she might *slaughter* all the cops that try to arrest you."

A tall, barrel-chested man with a matching Day of the Dead face strides up holding two cups of steaming apple cider and hands one to my mother.

"What's happened, lassie?" he asks with a heavy Scottish lilt to his voice. "What's all the commotion about?"

"Oh, Brennan, thank goodness." Mom takes a careful sip of her cider.

Brennan Gallagher is not only my mother's Day of the Dead compadre in skeletal arms, but he happens to be her boyfriend.

"Bizzy's done it again," she tells him. "You're right, we've got a situation on our hands with this one, and it is definitely getting out of control."

A situation on their hands with this one? Am I the *one*?

"Brennan?" I gawk up at him.

"I'm sorry, lassie." He shakes his head at me. "But I just call 'em like I see 'em."

I take a moment to frown at the two of them. "I'll accept your apologies in advance." I turn to my sister. "What else did Carrie Hazelman say about the deceased?"

Macy blows out a breath. "I don't know. She said something about suing the pants off of him. Or was it his jacket? People were trying to remove that, too. You got to admit, despite all that gunk on his face, he was a hottie."

She glances to where he lies just as a swarm of deputies

27

arrives on the scene and a crowd begins to swell. A mob of teenagers has their phones pointed at the poor guy, and it's becoming clear the crowds are fully aware of the fact a serious situation is at hand.

"Look." Macy points to a blonde dressed in a crimson robe. "There's Carrie now. Let's go over and offer our condolences."

I shake my head. "Why would she want our condolences if she was going to sue him?"

Georgie smacks me on the arm, and I hadn't even noticed she was standing there. "What kind of detective are you? Use it as a device to kick-start the investigation. We've got a body on the ground and a killer on the loose."

Macy nods. "She's right. That man practically collapsed on top of you, Biz. If that wasn't a hint from the universe to let you know it wants you to solve another homicide, I don't know what is."

"Fine." I look over at the blonde as she struggles to get as close to the body as possible while Jasper and Leo string up caution tape to create a broad perimeter. "Let's go." The three of us head on over, and Macy is the first to reach her.

"*Carrie.*" Macy offers the woman a smile. "I'm so sorry for your loss."

"Thank you." The blonde sniffs as she pulls her red robe tight, and I can't help but notice it looks luxuriously thick as if it might be velvet. The woman has a round face, full lips, and large blue eyes with nary a hint of crimson to imply tears were on the way. "At the end of the day, Barnabas and I were family."

"The two of you were family?" I ask, stunned by the revelation.

She nods. "Stepsiblings." She glances to the sky. "Or something of that nature."

Something of that nature?

Oh, who the hell cares? The blonde casts a dark look to the man on the ground. *He's dead, and that nightmare is all over with now. My goodness, I can finally breathe. I need to celebrate. I need to ditch this place and pull out a bottle of chilled champagne. I've been eying those bottles of Moet and Chandon Esprit du Siècle Brut Daddy has in his wine cellar. This is definitely the night to crack one open.*

"I'm sorry. I have to leave." She sniffs hard into her hand as if she were suddenly struck with grief. Someone get this woman an Oscar to go with that fancy bottle of bubbly. "I need to break the news to the rest of the family, of course."

"Of course," I say as I glance at her robe. I can't bear to look her in the eye after that champagne-laced diatribe.

"Oh"—she startles as she tugs at the velvet she's ensconced in—"do any of you need a hood for the ceremony?"

"What ceremony?" I ask.

She shakes her head. "I'm sorry. I thought you knew. But if you have to ask, I'm afraid you don't. And I'm not at liberty to divulge any details."

"That's my sister for you." Macy rolls her eyes as she strips the woman of her costume and quickly wraps it around her body. "I forgot my hood at home. Now, where were the girls meeting up again?" *You'd think Bizzy would know better by now. Even I know to play along rather than ask a stupid question.*

It was not stupid.

Carrie nods as if it was. "Out in the woods where they butt up against the pastureland. If you hurry, you can make the bloodletting."

"Bloodletting?" Georgie lifts a brow, suddenly interested in the conversation at hand. "You're not having that kind of fun without me. I've got a red wonky quilt in my shop. We'll grab it on the way, and I'll bundle up and join the fun." They link arms and take off just as Carrie melts into the crowd as well.

Bloodletting. Wonderful.

And Carrie Hazelman is off to celebrate this poor man's death—a family member no less.

I glance over toward the melee as deputies make room as the coroner's office arrives on the scene. Just past them, Griffin and Sabrina, the redhead I met earlier, congregate, so I head in their direction.

"Griffin, Sabrina," I say as I come upon them. "I'm sorry you had to see this." I nod to Griffin. "I'm guessing from your interaction earlier, he was your friend."

"He was." Griffin offers a pained smile. "I will always treasure our friendship." He casts a dark look to the man. "Barnabas and I were closer than brothers at times." *He knew all my secrets, and I knew all of his.* He shakes his head. "Tragic. He was so young."

"Thirty-two," Sabrina offers. *Same age as Justin.*

I offer a mournful smile her way. "I'm sorry. Did you know him as well?" I don't know who Justin is, but it's not uncommon for people to juxtapose one death against another.

Sabrina tips her head back, her cardinal locks shining like fire under the duress of the endless twinkle lights and streetlamps up above. "I guess you could say that." *I knew him well enough to know what a monster he truly was.* A smile flickers over her lips. "He's dead." *There's no point in rehashing any of the ways I knew him. Barnabas Casper was a wart on the rump of society, and now he's gone into the great unknown. I bet the flames are ready to greet him. I think I'll go over and have a few more of those free cupcakes in his honor. I wouldn't call it a celebration—more like a victory.* She offers Griffin a quick embrace. "Stop by the farm soon. I could use your company." Her eyes linger over his a moment too long. *With Barnabas gone, it's time I enjoy my life to the fullest—and that includes my love life, too. It's our time, Griffin.* She nods at him as if he can hear her. *And you know it, too.*

She takes off, and Griffin blows out a steady breath.

"Looks as if she's interested," I say. I don't know why I went there. A man has been killed, and I may have already spoken to the killer. Both Carrie and Sabrina seem more than thrilled by the fact Barnabas Casper is no longer breathing.

"She is." He shakes his head. "But I'm not." *I was up until I laid eyes on Bizzy Baker. This girl has got it going on. I should have figured. She's unstoppable in every department, brains and beauty included. What the hell was I thinking letting Mack Woods steer me away from her all those years ago? I may have been an idiot then, but I'm not letting Mack or anyone else stand in my way now.*

My mouth falls open.

Clearly, the death of his friend is clouding his judgment. He's forgotten all about the fact I'm a married woman.

Jasper steps up before I can remind him, and a breath of relief expels from me.

"Don't worry, Griffin. My husband is on the case," I say, wrapping an arm around Jasper's waist.

Really? Jasper muses. *He's hitting on you that hard that you had to remind him you were married?*

I give a covert nod his way.

Jasper growls over at the man, "Griffin, I'm afraid the death of your friend looks suspicious. I'm going to need you to cooperate. If the coroner agrees with my assessment, we might just have a homicide on our hands."

Griffin's chest expands twice its size. "A homicide?" he

balks. *Of course, it's a homicide. Anyone who knew the guy halfway could see this on the horizon, but I don't want to come across as arrogant in that department. The less knowledge I have of something nefarious, the better. I've got the bar and my company to think about. The last thing I need is to be dragged into an active homicide investigation. The press would have a field day with that one.*

I nod because I completely understand. As a business owner myself, I try to stay out of the homicidal limelight. *Try* being the operative word.

"You have my full cooperation, Detective." Griffin offers him a solemn nod. *And while he's out sifting for clues, I'll be keeping his bride company. And if I play my cards right, Bizzy will be my bride soon enough.*

I scoff at the thought. So much for thinking he had forgotten about my prior marital commitment.

I'd call Griffin a louse, but I still can't bring myself to judge him for his thoughts. It's not as if he's said any of that out loud. People can think the most outrageous thoughts, but those thoughts don't make them a bad person.

A sharp howl comes from our right, and we turn to find a scruffy man with dark hair and a matching beard. It's the same man I saw earlier, having what looked to be an argument with Barnabas.

"Don't mind him," Griffin says. "The guy is weird. Barnabas once told me, the dude actually thinks he's a werewolf."

Another howl emits from the man, sharper, inhumanly loud. And a part of me is suddenly convinced that he might be just that—a werewolf.

"Do you know him?" I ask, and Griffin shakes his head. "Barnabas told me his name once, can't recall it at the moment. But I do know that he and Barn had some strange dealings going on."

"Duly noted," Jasper says, his eyes still pinned over Griffin's. "And what about you? Did you have any strange dealings going on with the deceased?"

Griffin's chest bucks with a quiet laugh. *Well, well, it seems the good detective has a bit of a jealous streak. Good. I like a challenge.*

A challenge? The high school girl in me might be amused, but the woman presently married to Jasper Wilder isn't amused in the least.

"Barnabas and I were friends," he says. "Good friends. And fair warning—as hard as you're going to work to track down his killer, I'm going to work twice as hard right beside you." He glances my way. *And ten times as hard to steal back what should have been mine to begin with.* "I'll see you both around." He picks up my hand and kisses the back of it before dissipating into the crowd.

Jasper growls, "I don't need to be a mind reader to know he just threw down the gauntlet." He glares in the direction Griffin took off in. "He wants you back. Well, too bad. That's not happening. And he's not getting to the killer before I do, either." He lands a lingering kiss to my lips. "I'll be home late. Don't wait up." He takes off to tend to his business as a crisp breeze blows between us.

I hold myself as I look around at the curious crowd, the weeping women, and the teenagers taking pictures as if they were the morbid paparazzi.

Somebody killed Barnabas Casper, and I plan on getting to the killer before Griffin does—and if statistics prove anything, I'll most likely get to them before Jasper does, too. Although in this case, I think Jasper might actually be thrilled to have me by his side.

If Griffin keeps up his campaign to steal me away, Cider Cove might just have another killer on the loose—one I won't be turning in. Not that Jasper is capable of murder—yet.

But someone here tonight was capable of murder, indeed.

A wild cackle breaks out from somewhere deep in the crowd, and it sounds like pure evil. Cider Cove—*Spider* Cove was visited by evil tonight. And I'll do whatever it takes to track them down.

Halloween is around the corner. It's the scariest time of the year. And if anyone has something to fear, it's whoever thought it was a good idea to off Barnabas Casper.

The killer has a lot of things to fear right now—and one of them is me.

CHAPTER 4

*I*t's the very next morning after the carnage that took place during that ill-fated zombie walk. I'm standing in the middle of the Country Cottage Café, staring out the expansive windows at the stormy sea and the dark boil of clouds that linger over our tiny cove like a bruise.

The Maine coastline is magical any time of the year, but it holds a special, spooky appeal in the fall as the weather takes a turn for the bitter. The Country Cottage Inn sits nestled against a sandy cove, and the café I'm currently in butts right up against it. There's a large sunroom for diners to enjoy their meals, and outside there's a spacious patio with a full-service outdoor grill and bar. Although now that the weather is about to turn on us, I suppose I'll have to close those services down for the winter. Last spring was our first go-round with the outdoor grill, and it was a hit right through last month. But as the beachgoers slowed, so has business.

"Cupcake?" Emmie comes at me with a tray of her delicious spider-themed treats. Each one is covered with smooth white frosting and has a black spider web piped onto the top with black icing. Not only is the treat in keeping with the haunted holiday upon us, but the entire café is decorated to the hilt with ghosts, goblins, scarecrows, and pumpkins scattered around every inch of the place.

Of course, the menu didn't come out unscathed. There are pumpkin spiced pancakes, pumpkin spiced muffins, pumpkin spiced coffee, and even pumpkin spiced soup. There's hotter than hell chili, and mummified hot dogs—wrapped in strips of croissant dough—*eyeball* pizza, and monster pie enchiladas. That's just the tip of the scary menu options. Emmie has been planning these culinary Halloween horrors for months.

"How can I resist?" I say, snapping up a spider web cupcake to call my own just as her brother Jordy joins us and takes a treat for himself.

Jordy is a year older than both Emmie and me, and that puts us all in our late twenties. Jordy shares Emmie's dark hair and denim blue eyes.

He's a looker, the town playboy, and he also happens to be my ex-husband. Our marriage was over before you could snap your fingers. An impromptu trip to Vegas, bad booze, and an Elvis impersonator were involved. But our union was dissolved just as fast as my brother could snap his legal eagle fingers. Huxley had just graduated from law school—from interning at his specialty family practice—and I was his first case. He told me he wouldn't charge me so long as I didn't make it a habit of marrying for the fun of it. I promised him I'd not only swear off booze, but I'd swear off the entire state of Nevada just to be sure that fiasco never happened again.

"I've got an idea," Jordy starts.

Don't trust him, Fish yowls as she scampers this way and I quickly scoop her up.

The Country Cottage Inn was voted the most pet-friendly resort in all of Maine for the fifth year in a row, and my love of animals may have had something to do with that.

Weren't those the famous last words he said to you the night he took you to be his bride? Fish paws the air in his direction. *You keep your silly ideas to yourself, Jordy Crosby.*

She's correct about his famous last words. I've recanted the story to Fish so many times, she's holding onto more details than I am at this point.

I glance over at the counter where Georgie sits as she makes it rain bacon for both Sherlock and Nutmeg.

"Go on," I say to Jordy. "But just so you know, if you're planning on stealing me away from Jasper and making me your bride once again, you'll have to stand in line."

Emmie gasps. "He didn't!"

Emmie knows all about the fact Griffin was there last night. He said hello to her at the dessert table. I haven't had the chance to fill her in on the tawdry details just yet, but it looks as if she's quickly come to the right conclusion.

"He did." I nod. "Go on, Jordy."

Jordy has been the groundskeeper slash handyman here at the inn for as long as I've been running the place. At first, I was just the manager. But when the owner unexpectedly died —by the hands of a killer—he bequeathed the grounds to me in his will.

Jordy straightens in his jeans and dark green flannel. "You've got a lot of people filing into this town thanks to Mayor Woods and her love of all things creepy-crawly. On my way here, there was already a crowd on Main Street, and most of the shops haven't even opened yet. That giant pumpkin that's the size of a house? There's a line, sixteen deep just waiting to take their pictures with it. Main Street isn't going to be able to handle all that business. I say we eat up the overflow."

"Great idea," I tell him. "But how?"

"I know!" Emmie gasps. "I can bake haunted gingerbread houses, and we can sell them decorated and undecorated. We can even turn the sunroom into a decorating station. We'll make money hand over fist. The ingredients hardly add up to anything. And we can transition to Christmas-themed ginger-bread houses, seamlessly."

"Ooh, I love it," I tell her. "And I want one. I can't wait to put a haunted gingerbread house on my table."

Jordy shrugs. "That's nice and all, but I was thinking a little bigger. How about we turn the ballroom into a real haunted house?"

"The ballroom?" I ask. "Shouldn't a haunted house have more than one room to fill its victims with fear and regret?"

"It should," he says. "Leave the details to me. I've got a buddy who's a part-owner at the Halloween Stop in Edison. I bet I could get a good deal on everything we'll need to make this haunted house the scariest in all of Maine. I just need a budget and your golden credit card."

"We should do it." Emmie nods. "I bet we could get kids

from the drama departments at both the high school and at the community college to help out. And Georgie knows that makeup artist who worked on the zombie walk. We could charge five bucks for every person who wants to come in. If you have a hundred people coming through in a day, you'll make five hundred bucks. And we still have all of October to get through. That's a lot of money."

"No way," Jordy says. "We're charging *twenty* bucks a person, and I bet you'll have two hundred people per day. Trust me. We'll have the entire Eastern Seaboard coming up to visit once we get this scream-fest going."

"Okay," I say, and Fish covers her ears with her paws.

Honestly, Bizzy? Do you really want to encourage people to run and scream through our precious inn? Haven't we had enough carnage around here?

She has a point. But then, the inn could really use a cash infusion.

"We'll do it," I say firmly. "And once we're swimming in money, we won't be sorry. I hope."

Famous last words. Fish meows extra sharp to serve as a warning.

Jordy takes off to get going on the project just as my brother walks in with the cutest little pumpkin nestled in a carrier strapped to his chest.

Oh look, Bizzy. Fish looks over at them and chortles. *Uncle Hux put his baby in a cat carrier.*

I chuckle at the thought myself. I've put Fish in a baby carrier so many times she thinks it's proprietary to cats.

Both Emmie and I coo in unison at my sweet nephew as we speed that way. Mackenzie is here, too, but she's gone straight for the counter to put in an order for coffee.

"Oh my goodness," I coo extra loud as I take in the sleeping angel. He's only a couple of weeks old and still looks like a fairy from some dreamy place with that haze of innocence surrounding him. He has dark hair, and murky navy eyes, which happen to be sealed shut at the moment. He's wearing a soft white sweater and has on a pumpkin-shaped beanie, complete with green leaves and a stem sprouting from it.

"Huxley." Emmie sighs. "Do you just feel like the luckiest man on the planet?"

Hux gives a loose nod. "I'd feel even luckier if baby Mack believed in sleeping at night. He wants to be fed every other hour. And, of course, I've got to change him while he's up."

"You're doing all that on your own?" Emmie marvels, and I'm tempted to nudge her.

"Of course, he's doing all that," I say. "Mackenzie Woods has the maternal instincts of a python." I grimace over at my brother. "Sorry."

"No use in sugarcoating the truth," he says. "But just for your information, the python protects its young fiercely." He frowns over at Mackenzie as she collects her pumpkin spice latte. "I'm hoping her maternal instincts will kick in. And if not, I've got this." He lands a kiss to his precious boy's forehead. "I knew it would be an uphill battle, but what I wasn't prepared for was for there to be no war at all. It's as if baby Mack is a pet I've picked up, and Mackenzie expects me to have full control over the situation because I've brought it onto myself." He sighs. "Maybe so, to that last part, but I'll make sure Mack never feels unwanted or unloved."

My heart aches for both my brother and the baby.

Mackenzie enters our midst. "The Halloween Spooktacular is off to a rousing start." She frowns over at me as she blows on her coffee. "All right, good touch with the dead body this time. Usually, I wouldn't be so quick to praise you for such a brazen act of violence, in a crowd of thousands no less, but there wasn't a person in attendance last night who could stop talking about that body. There were even reports of ghostly sightings. It turns out, death is very good for business in the month of October. Try to keep your killings relegated to this spine-chilling month, would you?"

"Mackenzie," I hiss as I give a quick look around. "I didn't do anything to that poor man. And death is terrible at any time of year." I'd tell her I don't believe in ghosts either, but I've been visited by enough disembodied spirits to know there's more than a ghostly possibility Barnabas showed up again last night. But most likely it was just a rumor, or the wind, or both.

"Oh, quit your whining." Mackenzie sips her coffee. "We ran into Jordy on the way in, and he told us all about your haunted house money grab. You should be kissing my pointed stilettos that I thought of the idea to transform this town from drab to fab. Business should be brisk right through the holiday season. Not to mention the fact we're going all out on Halloween night itself. This entire town is going to blow up, just you wait and see."

Emmie moans, "Let's hope the universe isn't taking that literally. You're supposed to call out the positive things you'd like to have happen."

Mackenzie blinks. "So you're saying you're a witch now?"

"A witch!" Georgie howls as she hustles my mother in our direction. "Preppy and I were just talking about how boring our shop is compared to all the other terrifying places to visit on Main Street."

Mom and Georgie opened a quaint little shop last winter called Two Old Broads—the name was courtesy of my sister, but it's been a hit ever since. They primarily sell wonky quilts

—quilts made of long colorful strips of fabric with raw edges. They come in every shape and variety, from wedding dresses, tote bags, jackets, to pet products.

"That's a wonderful idea," Mom says as she scoops the baby out from Huxley's carrier. "Do you hear that? Your grandma is going to be a wicked witch!"

"Going to be?" Mackenzie muses.

"Mack," Hux snips. "Come on."

"You come on," Mackenzie snips right back. "I'm still picking wrapping paper out of the sofa from the impromptu baby shower she threw last month."

Any other person would have appreciated my mother's gift-giving efforts. But then, Mackenzie Woods has never been any other person. In fact, she's the exact reason I'm able to pry into other people's minds. After she pushed me into a whiskey barrel filled with water when we were thirteen, a few things came of it. One: I began to hear the private musings of others just as easily as I could hear the human voice. Two: I grew wary of large bodies of water. Three: I abhor confined spaces. And four: I grew wary of Mackenzie Woods as well. I let our friendship linger through high school, and even let her steal a handful of boyfriends before I finally cried uncle. Ironically, Griffin Duncan was the last man she stole. Or at least I think he was. Believe me, it was nothing I was trying to keep track of.

Speak of the devil...

Griffin waltzes into the café with a heady grin, a suit that makes him look as if he just stepped out of *GQ*, and enough white noise streaming from his gray matter to let me know he has something naughty on his mind—and I'm afraid it concerns me.

"Bizzy Baker." He pulls me in and lands a kiss just shy of

my lips. "You are a sight for sore eyes. I can't believe you own this entire inn. Over seventy rooms? Over three dozen cottages you rent out, to boot?"

"Don't forget the pet daycare center," Emmie adds. "Bizzy has a heart of gold for those born with and without fur coats."

Griffin's smile widens. "I would expect nothing less. And with this killer ocean view? You're sitting on a pile of money. Sorry, Mackenzie, but you were wrong. I think Bizzy is the most successful business person of our graduating class."

Mackenzie snorts. "She might look good on paper, but I suppose no one knows the truth but her accountant. What are you up to this afternoon, Griff? I've got a private tour of Spider Cove getting ready to launch. I'd love to include you in that number."

"I'm in," he says before looking my way. "How's the detective doing with the case? Any word?"

"It's still early," I tell him. "They're waiting for the coroner to determine the cause of death."

"I hope for everyone's sake it was natural." He sighs. "But if it's not, let me know as soon as possible. I think I'd point him straight to the person who had the biggest beef with the guy."

"Who would that be?" I ask, my voice lowered in an effort to tame my enthusiasm.

"Sabrina Chambers." He nods. "She just hated the guy, and I could never figure out why. At first, I actually thought she was interested in him—playing hard to get, that sort of thing. But it was too visceral. Anyway, I'm sure she had nothing to do with it. But I'd talk to her nonetheless."

"I'll pass it along if things take a dark turn with the coroner."

"Perfect," Mackenzie says as she leads him toward the

door. "We're off to see every inch of Spider Cove. Don't wait up."

"I'll be up, all right," Hux says, trying to take the baby from my mother, but she's putting up a fight.

"Well?" Georgie, says. "Are we off to track down the killer, or am I headed to Edison to buy a couple of pointed hats?"

I nod. "The inn has a sudden need for pumpkins."

Sherlock and Nutmeg run this way, and I give them both a quick scratch.

"Great news," I tell them. "We're headed to the Montgomerys' farm to pick out a few more pumpkins for the inn."

Sherlock barks and jumps. *You're going to love it there, Nutmeg. They don't mind if we run free, so long as we don't burn the place down.*

Last summer, Georgie and my sister burned the Montgomerys' barn to cinder. And just last month, I may have inadvertently stolen their entertainment from their fall festival and landed them as the key band right here at the inn. It was a total disaster through no fault of my own. And despite all of my profuse apologies, the Montgomerys still aren't all that thrilled with me. Macy was involved in that fall festival fiasco as well. It's safe to say Macy and Georgie are a dangerous duo ready to take down barns and friendships alike.

Here's hoping they let us back onto the property.

And here's also hoping I catch a killer while I'm picking out a pumpkin or two.

CHAPTER 5

*T*he Montgomery farm is set on a vast number of acres, not more than fifteen minutes from the Country Cottage Inn, and yet the air holds far less saline and far more country charm out this way. The orchards are to the left, there's the skeleton of a brand-new barn being erected straight ahead—in the exact spot Georgie and Macy inadvertently burned down the last one. And to the right, there's a pumpkin patch that goes on for miles as those happy orange globes dot the land in every shape and size. Throngs of people comb over the grounds in that direction as they take their time choosing just the right pumpkin for carving.

A large banner hangs over the arched entry to the farm that reads *Welcome to the Annual Halloween Festival!*

Carnival rides and games have been set up in the clearing to the left of the pumpkin patch, and a few of those rides make my stomach turn just watching them. Straight ahead there's an entire midway of games guaranteed to suck the change right out of your pockets and rows of food vendors selling everything from grilled and buttered corn to funnel cake.

I take a deep breath as soon as I let Sherlock and Nutmeg run out of the car. Fish insists that I hold her lest one of the roving beasts that lives on the property thinks it's a good idea to chase a cat, and I happen to agree with her. It's true. The farm has more than a handful of sweet, docile dogs that roams the grounds, but once they spot a furry feline they perk up and give a decent chase. In the past, Fish has played along and made them regret their chasing efforts, leaving the poor things panting, limping, and begging for both mercy and water, but today she didn't want to get chased right out of the investigation, so she asked if I'd carry her instead.

A car pulls up alongside of me, and both my mother and Georgie spill out of it.

Since Georgie insisted on coming along with me, and they still needed to get to Edison to buy their witchy Halloween costumes later, they took a separate car.

"I'm going to buy baby Mack his first pumpkin," Mom calls out with more than a little glee as she trots this way. "We'll buy some for the shop, too. And Mistletoe and Holly will each get their own."

Mistletoe and Holly are my mother's sweet cats. They're as much her children as my siblings and me.

They get their own pumpkins? Fish perks up at the thought. *Since when? I don't recall ever having a single pumpkin to call my own. I think Grandma is playing favorites.*

I want a pumpkin, too, Bizzy! Sherlock barks. *I want ten of the small ones that look like tennis balls.*

Tennis balls? Nutmeg quirks an ear. *I think I'd like a few of those myself.*

A laugh streams from me. "Don't worry." I give both Sherlock and Nutmeg a quick scratch behind the ears. "I'll pick up an entire slew of miniature pumpkins for the two of you."

And don't you worry, Bizzy, Fish mewls. *I just want one. A big one that you could carve for me, if you don't mind. I want it to look like a dog.*

"I would never leave you out of the pumpkin fun." I land a kiss to her forehead to emphasize the fact.

A dog? Sherlock cocks his head her way. *Why? So you could spray it whenever you like?*

Fish hisses down at him, *You know I don't spray. You're just trying to embarrass me in front of Nutmeg. If you must know, I thought we should put something scary out on the front porch this year to keep all of the candy beggars away. Last year, they pounded on our door at all hours, and then I had to listen to you bark all night. I figured if I had your face out there scaring them off, we might all get a good night's sleep.*

Sherlock lifts his furry little chin. *I am rather ferocious, aren't I?*

I'm not sure Fish meant it as a compliment, but I'm going to let sleeping ferocious dogs lie.

Come on, Nutmeg. Sherlock nudges at her. *Let's go pick out our tennis balls.*

They scamper off, and I'm about to clue my mother and Georgie in on my game plan when it comes to speaking with Sabrina when Melissa Montgomery walks past us, then backtracks once she sees us.

"Bizzy." She straightens with a look of mild horror on her face. Melissa is a friendly brunette with an easy smile and kind eyes—and yet at the moment, that easy smile is more of a frozen grimace, and those kind eyes are glazed over with sheer terror. "Hello, Ree, Georgie." She sighs hard as if acquiescing to some dismal reality in which her life's work goes up in smoke. "Welcome to the farm. Try not to destroy anything while you're here." Her lips swim as she says it, and it's more of a practical statement than anything rude. She speeds off with a look that suggests she's going to call for reinforcements. Can't say I blame her.

"We won't destroy anything," I say mostly to myself as I hold Fish tight.

"Look at that!" Georgie points to our right with marked enthusiasm, and her kaftan blows in the chilly breeze like an orange kite. "It's a pumpkin cannon."

Sure enough, just shy of the skeleton of the new barn, there's a pumpkin cannon spitting out an orange glorified squash toward a target about fifty feet out, much to the delight of the crowd.

"No," I say without hesitation. "Do not look, think, or go anywhere near that pumpkin cannon. Those things are dangerous. And if we're anything around here, we're dangerous ourselves."

"She's right," Mom says. "You saw that look on Melissa's face. You can bet your wrinkled patoot the security team here is going to monitor our every move. We'll be lucky if we don't get arrested before we pay for our goods."

"Security detail?" Georgie looks suddenly interested in causing a little chaos. "I bet they're beefy, brawny men with rock-hard abs and delicious buns of steel."

"Good grief." Mom glances skyward. "Now look what we've done. We've gone and whet her appetite for destruction."

Fish chuckles. *Do you think Georgie will find a way to launch herself out of that cannon? Should we take bets?*

I shake my head at my precocious little kitty. There have been far too many Georgie-inspired incidences for me to know that human cannonball theory of hers isn't entirely outside the realm of possibility.

Georgie waves my mother off. "I'm not the one with an appetite for destruction around here. It's you-know-who." She points my way. "I'd check your appetite for destruction at the door, Missy. Mama's hot toddie got cold feet once he found out you would be attending this little day trip. It turns out, our sexy Scotsman was afraid to come to the farm, because he thought you might have a little something to do with *him* buying the farm."

I gasp. "Is Brennan really afraid of me?" It's not like I had to ask. His roving thoughts have alerted me to as much in the past few months.

"Well..." Mom's mouth opens and closes. "I wouldn't say he was necessarily *afraid* of you. He just seems to find it highly —*coincidental*, that whenever you're around the odds of death and dying skyrocket."

Fish is right back to cackling. *He's right, you know. You're lucky you snagged Jasper when you did.* She straightens in my arms. *Come to think of it, you never stumbled upon a single body before he showed up on the scene. Quick, get rid of him and his little dog, too. You don't want your mother's relationship to suffer, do you? And think of all the future victims just lying in wait. I think we've just figured out how to kick crime in the rear —by kicking Jasper and Sherlock out on their rears.*

Hmm, now there's a theory I had never considered.

"I'm not kicking Jasper out," I tell her.

"What?" Mom inches back. "Who said anything about kicking Jasper out?"

"It's happening," Georgie moans. "The great unraveling. They say when a person starts to spontaneously argue with themselves they're just a moment away from taking a hatchet to their family members. I'll give Brennan the heads-up."

I roll my eyes.

Georgie knows full well I was responding to Fish. Georgie is one of the few people who knows all about my odd mind-reading quirk. She's just goading my mother in an effort to get a response out of her. It's her favorite pastime.

"Don't you dare tell him a thing, Georgie," Mom shouts it out like the threat it is. "The poor man is practically skittish at this point. He already expressed the fact he's afraid if he makes one wrong move with me, he's going to be hacked to pieces in his sleep."

Georgie nods my way. "He's already laid out the game plan for you, Bizzy. Now all you have to do is find someone to pin the blame on." She hitches her head toward my mother three times fast.

"Stop," Mom grouses as she cinches her purse over her shoulder. "I don't want to talk about Brennan or any of his irrational fears. It feels dirty, like I'm gossiping about my own boyfriend."

"You're right, Preppy," Georgie says as we make our way into the festival and do our best to dodge the killer clowns, pint-sized candy hoarders—dressed adorably from teddy bears to ninjas—and the odd roving group of teenagers with various stages of blood and guts marring their clothing. "We should gossip about someone else—someone like Mayor Woods."

Mom grunts, "Don't get me started on that girl."

"Did someone say gossip?" a familiar female voice calls out and we turn to see Macy trotting her way over. "And about Mayor Woods? Don't you dare start without me."

"We are not gossiping about Mackenzie," I say. "She's the mother of our nephew," I remind my sister.

Macy's blonde hair looks a shade lighter, any trace of her dark roots gone. My guess is, she's just come from the salon.

"What's with the stop at the Halloween festival?" I ask her.

"I brought Candy over to pick out a pumpkin. It's her first Halloween with me, and we're going to do it in style. Besides, I had to meet with Melissa. She's a part of the Red Riding Hood Society." Her fingers clamp over her lips. "I keep forgetting it's a secret." She gives a devious wink of delight. "Just forget that I ever mentioned it."

My mouth falls open. "Are you talking about that group of girls who were wearing red robes and chanting? Is that what they're called? The Red Riding Hood Society?"

"Girls?" she balks. "We like to think of ourselves as women, Bizzy. And I'm not at liberty to divulge any sensitive information about the society of which any of you know nothing about. Now back to Mackenzie. Did you hear she's got herself a boyfriend?"

"She does not," I say.

Fish mewls, *Oh, I think she does.*

Mom nods. "I didn't have to hear. I saw the whole thing play out with my own eyes. She's gallivanting up and down Main Street with that Griffin person as we speak."

"Griffin Duncan?" Georgie gasps. "Bizzy, that Mackenzie Woods is trying to steal your man for old times' sake. You're not going to let her get away with it, are you?"

A man with a chainsaw runs our way, screaming, and the three of us simply step right past him. You might say my regular run-ins with real killers have desensitized the entire lot of us.

"Yes, I'm going to let her get away with it." I shake my head at the thought of fighting for Griffin. "I mean, she's not dating him, and he's not my boyfriend. Both Mackenzie and I are married women. I can assure you, neither of us is interested in Griffin Duncan anymore."

"You might not be," Mom huffs. "But Mackenzie? Her, I'm not so sure about. She practically left Huxley holding the baby bag. The only interaction she has with her child is when she asks Huxley to take *it* out of the room so she can think straight. Hux has been sleeping on the couch with the bassinet next to him because she still refuses to set up a proper nursery. I don't think she plans on keeping Hux or the baby."

"I think we need to cut her some slack," Macy says. "We knew Mackenzie was going to be a hands-off mom because she told us as much. Some women just aren't cut out for dirty diapers, sleepless nights, and an endless stream of baby vomit. Mackenzie Woods has basically instated the same mothering plan I would have developed myself. She's the one that carried the kid for nine long months. I say let the man that got her into that baby pickle to begin with take over for the next nine."

"That's what I did." Georgie winks her way.

"Lovely," Mom mutters. "Let's get this pumpkin show on the road so we can get out to Edison and shop until our witchy hearts drop, then get back to the store before Juni gives everything away for free." *It wouldn't be the first time. Last month, when she told me that we had sold out of everything and she needed to close early, I actually thought it was a good thing. She sure taught me a lesson.*

I bite down on a smile.

Juni is Georgie's daughter. They look the same sans a few wrinkles. Juni was actually married to my father for all of five minutes. She was wife number three or thirty-three. I've never kept track of my father's matrimonial pursuits—except for his latest dalliance in tying the knot. He's currently married to Jasper's mother. Neither Jasper nor I am holding our breath as far as how long it might last. We're just hoping we survive the fallout.

We thread our way through the mob and finally make it to the pumpkin patch laid out before us like an orange speckled nirvana for people of all ages. I spot Sherlock, Nutmeg, and Candy trotting through the expansive rows, nudging their selections with their noses before moving on to the next pumpkin down the line.

Just past the pooches, I spot my mark.

Sabrina Chambers stands happily chatting with a family of three as she helps load a pumpkin into their wagon. Her crimson locks are tied back into a ponytail, and she's wearing a red and black buffalo plaid flannel over jeans. There's a pleasantness about her as she gives an easy laugh and waves the family off.

"You ladies busy yourselves with pumpkins," I whisper. "In fact, Georgie, why don't you go get a wagon and fill it with whatever the three of you need? I'll pay for everything." So long as they leave my suspect alone.

"I'll get the wagon," Macy volunteers. "And then I'll find a buff ranch hand to pull it for me."

"Atta girl," Georgie says as she takes off. "Face it, Preppy. You may not get a grandkid out of that one, but she'll deliver hundreds of potential sons-in-law."

Mom balks, "*Potential* being the operative word. I don't think I'll get a wedding out of her either. Come on, let's go find a few pumpkins before all the good ones flee the scene."

I'm with her, Bizzy. Fish lashes me with her tail. *Let's talk to our suspect before she flees the scene.*

"I'm on it." I traipse through a small dirt trail while traversing pumpkins of every size and nearly tripping over a vine or two. "Excuse me?" I call out just as Sabrina is about to walk in the opposite direction, and she turns my way. "Hello! I'm looking to pick up a couple dozen pumpkins for the Country Cottage Inn. I'm Bizzy Baker Wilder, the owner there."

"Oh wow!" Her face brightens. "That's wonderful. I can help you with that."

"Perfect," I say, panting as I come upon her.

Sabrina coos at my feisty feline, "Aren't you the cutest?" She gives her a little pat over the back. "I used to have a cat just like you when I was growing up. Her name was Tiger, and she was always getting after our dog. But at the end of the day, I'd like to think they really loved each other."

I'd like to think that, too—regarding my own little tiger.

"Her name is Fish," I tell her. "And some days I'm convinced she thinks she's a tiger." I inch back, feigning surprise. "Hey? Didn't we meet yesterday?"

Fish fans me with her tail. *Your acting skills have markedly improved over the years. But please don't eschew the inn for Hollywood. If I would have complimented Sherlock like that, he would have slung a sack of bacon around his neck and headed off for the railroad. Hey? Maybe I'll do just that. Wish me luck,*

Bizzy. It looks as if I'll be doing a little acting myself this afternoon.

I sigh because it's clear I'll have to monitor the situation. A runaway dog is the last thing I need. Although, I suspect the bacon trail he'd leave behind would lead me straight to him.

"Wait a minute..." Sabrina gives a few quick blinks. "I think we did meet."

"Griffin introduced us." I nod. "It was a horrible thing that happened yesterday, don't you think?"

Horrible? She lifts a brow. *I wouldn't go that far.*

"Did you know the deceased?"

She nods quickly. "Oh, I knew him well. Our fathers used to be friends way back when. They were lawyers at the same firm."

"Barnabas' dad was a lawyer?" Macy told me last night that Carrie said Barnabas was worth billions. And yet his father is a lawyer? A billionaire lawyer? Huxley is an attorney and he's earning far from millions, let alone *billions*. I wonder where the billions are coming from?

She nods. "Yup. He and my dad actually owned the firm along with a couple of others, but things went south for them and our families were basically at war for a few years. It was pretty horrible."

At war? Fish's ear twitches. *That sounds like a motive for murder to me.*

Me, too.

"A war, huh?" I muse. "Can I ask what would sponsor a war between friends?"

A myriad of things can do just that. I need her to narrow down the field.

Sabrina takes a huge breath and arches her back. She has dirt under her nails and a smear of it on her face as if she's already had a long day's work and it's hardly noon. My guess is, pumpkin farming isn't nearly as cute as it looks.

"You know, it sounds a lot more far-fetched than you'll ever believe. My dad and mom were going through a divorce, so my dad leased a property that Barnabas' father owned. We lived in that house for a good year before his father started doing some shady things."

"Shady things?" I tip my head. "He doesn't sound like he was a very good friend to your father."

"He wasn't. Well, I take that back. He was a great friend until my father caught him going at it with the wife of another partner at the firm. That's when things took a turn for the worse. You see, my dad actually had a conscience. He told Barnabas—*Senior*— that he was going to have to stop the affair and fess up to their buddy, but Barnabas Senior thought he was out to ruin him, so he decided to ruin my father first. We should have seen his fury on the horizon, they were both fiercely competitive. Neither of them was willing to back down. But the truth is, nobody could have anticipated what happened next."

"What happened?" both Fish and I say in unison.

"Barnabas *Senior* resorted to petty behavior, and lots of it. He told everyone at the firm that my father had stopped paying on his lease. He said we were squatters. And just as bad as that, he sent handymen in to act as spies and they took pictures of the inside of our home—the most unflattering pictures. My brother and I had just done a little spring-cleaning and threw a pile of clothes and old junk into the hall. Well, Barnabas showed those pictures to the people at the firm and labeled us hoarders in addition to being squatters. My father was so humiliated. It was a horror show."

"That's terrible."

"It would have been if that was the end of it. But it got worse. He paid someone to subscribe my father's cell number and his email address to a bunch of spam websites. They also scheduled my father at all the massage parlors from Maine to Manhattan. It was some real sophomoric stuff. I heard him tell my father once that it was all harmless fun." *But it wasn't harmless—and it wasn't fun. It was far from it.*

"I'm sorry to hear it. I bet that affected your relationship with Barnabas—Junior."

Her lips crimp a moment. "I guess you could say it did." *I'm not getting into the fact we dated—that we viewed ourselves like some rebel version of Romeo and Juliet. It was all in my mind. I was a fool.* An image of a young man blinks through her mind, and she quickly shuts it down. "Anyway. Barnabas dropped dead out of the blue yesterday. That was weird." She sighs again. *Not so weird when you pull back the curtain, but I'm not about to get into that either.*

My eyes widen a notch.

"Do you know what happened?" I ask.

"I don't know." She brings her thumb to her lips a moment as she considers it. "But he was young. I mean, sure, his body could have malfunctioned in any number of ways, but it's doubtful. Barnabas had some enemies. He had that whole twisted family drama that plagued him." She shakes her head. "I always felt sorry for him in that respect."

"Wow, what kind of family drama?"

Her mouth opens to speak just as Sherlock, Nutmeg, and Candy run this way, barking as if their tails were on fire.

Bizzy! Sherlock howls. *We need your help, quick! We have a real emergency.*

Not now, you big buffoon, Fish yowls. *Can't you see we're investigating? This woman is just getting to the good part.*

It's true. I'm sure Sherlock's emergency can wait just a minute.

Sabrina groans as she looks past me, "I'm sorry, Bizzy. It looks like I've got a situation I need to handle. But you could probably ask Griffin about Barnabas' family drama. They were great friends, and he probably knows more about it than I do." She darts off, and I turn around to see what the emergency is when I spot a flash of an orange kaftan sticking out of the pumpkin cannon. The cannon is at least nine feet long and five feet off the ground.

"GAH!" I toss Fish in the air without meaning to as I bolt in that direction.

I told you it was a real emergency, Sherlock barks as all three dogs speed ahead of me.

He wasn't kidding.

Not only is Georgie seemingly stuck inside that cannon, but my mother is strapped to the top of it like a missile trying to push her out, and Macy has grabbed ahold of Georgie's bird legs. I'm not entirely sure if Macy is trying to pull her to safety or jam her farther into the bed of the cannon. You never know with my sister.

"What's happening?" I shout as I burst through the crowd amassed to gawk at the sight. "Where's the staff?"

"They went to get the butter," Macy grunts. "Don't just stand there, grab a leg."

I do as I'm told and give a hard yank.

"Georgie!" I shout. "What were you thinking?"

"A cat ran in there," Macy grunts again. "And she dove in to save it."

"They had just loaded it," Mom shouts from the top of the contraption. "And Georgie swears she saw an orange tabby run in after it. I tried to tell her they threw in another pumpkin, but she wasn't having it!"

"Oh my stars," I cry out as I give Georgie a tug, but she proves to be immovable.

"I've got the butter!" Sabrina shouts as she barrels this way with a few beefy men outfitted with toolboxes in each hand.

"Hang on, Georgie! They're coming with drill bits!" Mom shouts.

"Drill bits?" The sound of Georgie's garbled voice comes from inside the contraption, and soon her entire body begins to wiggle and jiggle in a panic.

The cannon starts to spin to the right then left, and before we know it, centripetal force takes over and both Macy and I lose our grip on Georgie's legs.

The rocket lurches hard to the left, and Georgie gets suctioned out of it with a popping sound like the unscrewing of a cork. The machine flops backward, and Mom hangs on for dear life as another loud explosion goes off and two large orange whoppers blow out of the front of it.

We watch, mesmerized, as the pumpkins fly across the sky, over the crowd, the games, the rides, and they head straight for the skeletal barn, hitting it just right at the top of a support beam.

A loud creaking sound emits from the structure. A hard moan comes as the wood beams wobble hard to the left, then right.

The entire crowd lights up with screams as people move away from the unstable display, and we watch in horror as what would have been the barn tips slow and lazy as a yawn before flopping onto its side.

"Run!" I shout as Macy and I help our mother off the

destructive contraption. I scoop up Fish, and the dogs follow us as we make a break for the parking lot.

Georgie gasps as she catches up to us. "I guess you were right, Preppy. It wasn't a cat. It was another pumpkin. Go figure."

"I've been telling you for months you need to get your eyes checked," Mom screeches as she fumbles for her keys and unlocks the car. "Now get in and let's head down to the Halloween shop. Try not to topple that place, too." She nods my way. "I'll have Huxley contact the Montgomerys on our behalf. It's best we let tempers cool before we try to make this wrong, right. We'll see you later."

She hops into the car and Georgie does the same. "Stop by the shop sometime and be prepared to be afraid, very, *very* afraid." She belts out a perfectly witchy cackle as they speed off of the lot.

"Come on, Candy," Macy calls her trusty pooch. "We'd better make haste before they throw us in the pokey." *And I can't risk missing the next meeting of the Red Riding Hood Society. We're smoking toad venom. It's the new* it *thing in Holly-wood, and I'm not going to miss it.*

"Macy," I hiss. "When is this next meeting of that Red Hat Society taking place?" Hood/hat, whatever.

"Two days from now. And believe me, if you knew what this thing was really about, you'd have thought I dreamed up this society myself." She gives a quick wink and speeds out of the lot herself.

"They're going to smoke toad venom?" I shake my head. "I couldn't have heard her right."

The sound of a multitude of angry voices drifts this way like a storm cloud, and I turn to see a mob heading this way and they look every bit ready to tar and feather me.

"Quick!" I shout as I open the door to my sedan. "Get in the car!"

Ladies first. Sherlock barks, and Nutmeg jumps in and he's quick to follow.

What about me? Fish shouts. *I'm a lady, too, you know.*

I don't bother informing Sherlock that I'm one myself. Instead, I seal them in and hop behind the wheel, and the four of us laugh like banshees as we speed all the way back to the inn.

Poor sleep-deprived Huxley has yet another mess to clean up with the Montgomerys on our behalf.

Sabrina suggested that I talk to Griffin about Barnabas' family, and I plan to do just that. Not only do I know where to find him, but I bet he'll be eager to tell me whatever it is I want to know.

Let's hope he doesn't read anything into it.

Although something tells me he will.

But if it brings a killer to justice—spending a little time with my ex is a small price to pay.

Here's hoping Jasper sees it that way, too.

CHAPTER 6

The Country Cottage Inn is a behemoth structure comprised of blue cobblestones covered with ivy. The walkways around the facility are comprised of blue cobblestones as well, and those, along with the cottages that dot the property, give this place a fairy-tale appeal.

Sherlock barks as we head toward the entry of the inn. *Didn't I say Georgie would get shot out of a cannon?*

You called it! Nutmeg barks and jumps.

No, he didn't, Fish mewls. *I called it. I was the one who suggested we take bets. Tell them it's true, Bizzy. I can't stand the defamation the canines demand to propagate.*

Sherlock leaps up and nips at her tail. *You may have said it, but I was thinking it.*

"We all were thinking it," I say as I take in the entry to the inn with its fall leaves, the excessive amount of spider webs, real and synthetic, the sinister-looking scarecrow, and the plethora of mums and pumpkins clustered around the mouth of the entrance.

Fall is my favorite time of year, pumpkin spice everything, crisp autumn breezes, and my secret desire to be scared silly playing out at every turn.

No sooner do I step inside the inn than a beady-eyed, hairy, scary werewolf jumps out at me and I toss Fish right out of my arms and scream.

The perpetrator rips the mask off his head, and I find my coworker, Grady Pennington, laughing like a fiend.

"Not funny," I say, barreling past him. The inside of the inn is comprised of dark mahogany and distressed gray floors. A grand staircase sits to my right, the dining hall to my left, the grand room to the right of that, and a marble reception counter sits straight head.

Behind the counter stands Nessa Crosby as she finishes up with a guest before joining Grady as they chuckle on my behalf.

Both Grady and Nessa started working at the inn while they were in college and they've stayed on post-graduation. They're two of my most trusty—and apparently, shifty employees. They also happen to be dating. It's relatively new, but I'm keeping an eye out for cracks in the foundation should one of them decide to leave the inn if things go south. But I'd double their pay to keep them. I value them both that much.

Nessa is a pretty brunette dressed as a naughty French maid. And Grady, the dark-haired Irish looker, is one werewolf everyone should be wary of.

Fish hops up onto the reception counter, while Sherlock teaches Nutmeg how to greet the guests at the door. It just so happens that Fish and Sherlock are my best furry employees.

"What's the deal, Bizzy?" Grady's countenance quickly sobers. "Jordy's been transforming that ballroom into a disaster zone all morning. It's truly terrifying."

Nessa nods. "The haunted house is already almost finished. He's got an army of people in there. Are you sure blood and gore is something the inn needed more of?"

Fish yowls, *I'm with Nessa. It's as if we're asking for a massacre to take place.*

Heaven forbid.

"Speaking of terrifying." Grady tosses a headband my way with a pair of jack-o'-lanterns bobbing on the antennae blooming from it. And each happy pumpkin has a pair of bat wings stemming from it. "You need to lead by example, Bizzy. Costumes every day, all day, remember?"

Those were the exact words I told the staff just last week.

"Thanks," I say, pressing the headband into place, and my temples begin to throb on cue.

Nessa comes around the counter and quickly puts on a couple of miniature rainbow clown wigs on Sherlock and Nutmeg, along with giant red bowties with yellow polka dots.

I don't like the fact she's making a clown out of me, Sherlock growls.

"Easy, boy," Grady tells him. "We're all in the same boat for the next few weeks." He digs a doggie treat out of the jar I keep on the counter and tosses one to each of the ornery pooches.

Nutmeg barks with glee. *I'll wear the wig as long as you like. Just keep the treats coming.*

Grady tosses another handful of biscuits their way. "That's how I feel about this place. Just keep the paychecks coming."

I bite down on a smile because Grady read Nutmeg's mind regardless of the fact he's incapable of doing so.

Emmie strides this way dressed as Little Bo Peep with a platter full of her spider web cupcakes in hand, and Nessa, Grady, and I don't waste any time in snatching one right up.

I take a bite of the rich chocolate cupcake with its creamy vanilla frosting and moan.

"Oh wow, these are good." I give her an approving nod. "How about we track down that wily brother of yours and see how the transformation is going?"

Emmie and I head in that direction, along with my furry companions, and I tell her all about my misadventures at the Montgomerys' farm.

"Geez," she groans. "Take another cupcake." She shoves the platter my way and I do as I'm told. "You're going to need the sustenance when the Montgomerys slap you with a restraining order."

"Now there's something I didn't think of."

We step into the ballroom, and both Sherlock and Nutmeg start in on a barking spree at the melee before us.

The cavernous room has already been parceled off with tall partitioned walls and black curtains. Scattered around are a pile of pumpkins, skeletons, nefarious looking gloves with nine-inch razors for fingernails, hockey paraphernalia, and enough terrifying masks and costumes to outfit all of Maine.

Jordy comes this way with a pair of horns on his head and a devilish smile on his lips.

"We should be done setting up by evening." He snags a cupcake off Emmie's platter. "I've got the drama department from three different schools filling in the monster blanks and we should be up and running by tomorrow night."

"Tomorrow night?" I balk. "That's insanity."

Fish scampers into my arms. *This entire display is insanity. This is going to be very scary—too scary for my blood. But I suppose that's what will bring in the big bucks.*

I nod over at Jordy. "You're off to a creepy start. Keep up the good work."

A wild cackle breaks out from behind and we turn to find a woman with a green face, a tight black dress, obscenely high heels, and a black pointed hat. I recognize the witch despite her sickly flesh. It's Camila Ryder—Jasper's ex-fiancé.

"Camila is working for us, too." Jordy holds out an arm and she nestles into it as if she belongs there.

"A witch, huh?" I muse as I look at Jordy. "I see you've hired a professional."

"You're hilarious," she growls.

Camila is tall, has chestnut hair with a body of its own, and a body that speaks its own language, literally.

While she was engaged to Jasper, she decided to cheat on him with his best friend, Leo, thus putting a damper on Jasper and Leo's relationship for years—not to mention severing her engagement. But now, Leo is happily married to Emmie, and I have Jasper all to myself. I guess at the end of the day, we can all thank Camila's idiocracy for our happily-ever-afters.

"So"—she lifts a shoulder my way—"rumor has it, you,

Bizzy Baker, have a boyfriend. And, since turnabout is fair play, I call dibs to be Jasper's side-piece."

"What? No," Emmie protests for me like the good best friend she is.

Fish hisses at the witch before us. *You stay away from Jasper, or I'll claw your green nose right off. If the oaf makes Bizzy happy then I'll tolerate him for as long as I have to.*

"Thank you," I whisper to her.

I think.

Camila waves Emmie off while looking my way. "Macy told me all about how your high school boyfriend zipped back into town, hoping to sweep you off your feet. Duncan Griffin." She shimmies her shoulders as she says his name and I don't bother telling her she has it backward. "He sounds handsome. Macy said he was h-o-t-t-e-r than hell." Leave it to Camila to spell out the wrong word. But then, she was probably just trying to honor her homeland. "In fact, I was just at your sister's shop where she happened to extend an invite to a very exclusive club." She inverts her lips. *Macy warned me not to tell Bizzy anything about it. She's right, Bizzy is too uptight to understand the common woman's desire to get her hands on a werewolf for the night.* She sucks in a quick breath and clamps her hand over her green mouth.

My own mouth falls open.

A werewolf?

I try to play it off as if I'm gasping at a group of teenage girls who just strode in looking like they could play extras in the Broadway musical *Cats*.

While Camila was dating Leo, all those eons ago, she got it out of him that he could read minds. Then one day, about a year or so ago, she saw Leo and me having a rather intense conversation without the use of our lips and she surmised the same about me, although I've never admitted as much to her.

"Never mind." She gives me a stern look before looking at Jordy. "I was going to ask you to be my date for the Monster Ball on Main Street, Halloween night, but now that I have my Jasper, you're off the hook for now."

"You're still on the hook," I tell him. "Stay away from Jasper," I say to Camila and she cackles right in my face. We both know she can't stay away from him. She's not only obsessed with him, but she's the secretary down at the homicide division in Seaview. And you can bet Camila's green bottom that was very much by design.

"So what's with the case you're working on?" she asks. "Headed anywhere fun?"

"No, actually. I have to speak with Griffin. He knew the deceased. They were friends."

"*Ooh.*" Camila is right back to rocking her shoulders seductively. "Sounds like a hot date is about to go down."

"No hot date," I inform her. "In fact, I'm going to head over to his cottage and see if I can't buy him a cup of coffee. Nothing more, nothing less."

Sherlock barks up at me. *Don't do it, Bizzy. I saw the way that man was looking at you. He looks at you the way I look at bacon. He's going to gobble you up the first chance he gets and you'll disappear. I'd miss you something awful, too.*

Goodness. Fish rolls her eyes. *Bizzy can handle him. I've seen plenty of men look at Bizzy as if she were bacon, and she hasn't been gobbled up yet. She's not going anywhere.* She looks up at me. *Just in case, maybe borrow Thor from Georgie.*

Thor is Georgie's handgun. And neither Georgie nor I should be handling Thor. He has a propensity to go off on his own—sort of like Camila.

Jordy shakes his head. "He won't be there."

Emmie makes a face. "Mack must have hidden him good. She probably has him staying at her place—in the room the nursery should have been in, just to keep him away from you."

"Nope." Jordy shakes his head. "I just saw him and Mackenzie in Edison. She said they were having lunch, then taking in a movie."

"Lunch and a movie?" Emmie hooks a brow my way. *That's exactly the move she pulled when she stole him away from you the first time.*

I give my bestie a dirty look.

"She's not stealing him from me. He's not mine to begin with." I don't mind one bit making that declaration out loud. "I'll track him down for dinner."

"Dinner?" Camila snorts. "Now if that doesn't scream *date*, then I don't know what does. I'd better get to the station. Don't worry, Bizzy. I'll make sure Jasper doesn't eat alone tonight!" She cackles as she heads out the door.

"I'm going to text Griffin," I say, snapping up another spider web cupcake. "And we're not going on a date. It's all a part of the investigation."

"You keep telling yourself that," Jordy teases as I take off for the reception counter.

I look Griffin up in the roster of guests and jot his number right into my phone.

I send a text asking if we could meet up this evening, and he wastes no time in texting right back.

You beat me to the punch. How about dinner at Lucky Thirteen? I'm just dying to wine and dine you. Let me do it in style. Tonight at seven. You in?

I text right back. *I'm in. I'll meet you later at Lucky Thirteen.*

Can't wait. He annunciates it with a kissing emoji.

I can't wait either—to catch a killer.

Here's hoping Griffin can point me in their direction.

I can't wait to hear all about Barnabas Casper's twisted family drama.

CHAPTER 7

*T*he autumn night air is bitingly chilly as I hop into my car to head to Edison.

My phone bleats, and it's a text from Jasper.

Are you up for date night? I can pick up Chinese and afterwards we can volunteer to be Jordy's first victims at the haunted house. Camila says it's just about ready for liftoff. Ready to have the pants scared off of you? That

would give me a head start for what I have planned for the rest of the night.

I bite down on a smile as I text right back.

I'd love to, but I have a previously scheduled date night that's getting in the way. I'm leaving now to meet Griffin for dinner at Lucky Thirteen out in Edison. Care to crash the party?

The dancing ellipses pop up on my screen.

Darn right I'm crashing that party. See you soon.

I toss my phone into my purse and peer into the crack in the curtains to see Sherlock, Nutmeg, and Fish all cuddled up on the sofa together. I left the television on the Animal Planet and fed them an extra big dinner full of treats—bacon for Sherlock and Nutmeg, and those Tuna Delight biscuits that make Fish mooney-eyed.

I let Jordy know I'd be out for the night, and that if he needed anything not to hesitate in messaging me. I'm not entirely comfortable with the inn being overrun with lunatics with chainsaws and crazed-looking killer clowns.

He said he'd do a dry run for an hour before he started selling tickets at the door. I'm not sure how he got the word out, but the parking lot is already at capacity with what looks to be mostly teenagers.

I should be at the inn, babysitting all of Cider Cove High, not running out to have dinner with my ex. This is all the killer's fault. Which makes me twice as angsty to track them down and quick.

Here's hoping I can get all the info I need out of Griffin—and something tells me I can get just about anything out of Griffin Duncan.

The trip to Edison is a smooth one, and I manage to find

parking not too far from the establishment that Griffin owns with his ex.

Lucky Thirteen is a large brown brick building with a spinning neon sign of a four-leaf clover with the number thirteen tucked inside it. A steady stream of bodies make their way inside, and each one of them is wearing a Halloween costume.

I frown as I head inside myself, suddenly feeling underdressed for the party.

Brick walls, stained concrete floors, loud country music, and the scent of grilled burgers greet me. Tables hug the periphery while vampires, werewolves, and naughty princesses sway on the dance floor.

It looks like a giant Halloween party is taking place as orange lanterns with jack-o'-lantern faces and a plethora of spider webs hang from the ceilings. A giant black cat—at least five feet tall—with glowing red eyes sits next to the register, and I make a note to order one for the inn. Fish would love it. Sherlock? Not so much, but it's so cute I just need to have it.

A redhead dressed as a cavewoman with a bone spiked through her disheveled hair comes at me with a smile.

"Welcome to Unlucky Thirteen. My name is Greta. We serve the best surf and turf in town. Not only do we offer grass-fed beef, but we hand-select our own seafood right down to the organic seaweed." She bounces with pride as she says it. "Dining alone tonight?" She winks. "We're changing the name from Lucky to *Unlucky* Thirteen the month of October."

"It's a booming trend," I bubble with a laugh. "I'm actually meeting someone for dinner—Griffin Duncan?"

She inches back, the smile quickly dissipating from her lips. *This is the hot date he was bragging about? She doesn't look like his typical fare. She looks too bookish to be a hussy, but then, 'tis the season for people to run around in disguises. This is probably hers.*

My lips part as I take her in. Did she just call me a hussy?

Wait a minute.

"Greta, you wouldn't happen to be Griffin's ex-wife, are you?"

Ex-wife? She frowns. *We've hardly filed the papers, and that louse is already selling himself as free and single. Eh. Who am I to ruin his good time? I'll go along with it for now. But neither of them is getting off easy tonight.*

"I am." She nods. "And Griffin is free to date whomever he likes." *Why should he change his behavior now?*

I gasp a little.

Did Griffin cheat on this poor woman?

"Follow me," she grunts, snapping up a couple of menus and leading me to a small table near the bar. She slaps the menus onto the table and aggressively pulls out a chair, but before I can take a seat, a handsome cowboy with a devilish gleam in his eyes shows up.

"Bizzy Baker." Griffin waggles his brows as he says my name—or at least part of my name. "This is for you." He thrusts a pink cowboy hat my way.

"Oh wow, thank you," I say, taking it from him and pressing it over my head. "I had no idea I should have worn a costume. I was feeling a little naked."

Greta rolls her eyes. *And knowing Griffin, she'll be feeling a lot more naked in just a few hours. I should spit in their food.*

Spit in my food?

Good luck getting me to take a bite.

"I'll be back to take your orders." She scowls at the two of us before taking off.

Griffin winces. *I wonder if Greta introduced herself? Hopefully not. The less Bizzy knows about that disaster, the better. Besides, tonight isn't about the soon-to-be last Mrs. Duncan—it's about the future Mrs. Duncan.* A smile spreads over his face. *And I'll do everything in my power to make sure that's Bizzy. I may have let her slip away from me once, but I'm not letting it happen again.*

My mouth squares out.

"I'm sorry." He tips his ear my way. "It's so loud in here, I'm afraid I didn't hear you."

"Oh, I was just admiring the place." And the size of your ego. "This place is really happening. It's something else." So is Griffin's imagination.

Did I not make it clear that I was married? Where is Jasper, anyway?

I give a quick glance around.

"It *is* quite the happening place," he says, taking up my hand. "How about we work up our appetites? A quick dance?"

He nods to the dance floor as he moves us that way, and before I know it, we're moving to the music. Thankfully, it's a fast song. I plan on keeping my limbs moving and as far away from him as possible.

This won't do. Griffin frowns as he signals to someone in the corner, and I crane my neck to see a DJ nodding this way.

The song ends abruptly, and something far moodier, and markedly slower, takes over instead.

Wonderful.

"Wonderful." He winks my way as he pulls me in tight. *This is more like it.* His hands dip low.

"Oh wow," I say, reflexively pulling his arms right back up again. "If I didn't know better, I'd think you switched up the music on purpose."

75

Griffin knocks his head back and laughs. "You're onto me, Bizzy. I tell you, the dumbest thing I ever did was let Mackenzie Woods steal me away from you." *She put in an honest effort this afternoon as well, but I'm not here to reopen old wounds or to talk about anyone but Bizzy and me.*

That's what he thinks. We'll be talking about Barnabas soon enough. I hope.

And what is the deal with Mackenzie, anyway? Did she really put in an honest effort to steal Griffin for herself this afternoon? Here's hoping that's just more of Griffin's ego talking. Although knowing Mack, I'm not so sure.

"Yes, well." I shrug. "Once Mackenzie Woods sets her eye on something, there's hardly any stopping her from getting what she wants. But alas, she's a married woman now—as am I." Take that.

A growl of a laugh rumbles from him, and his hands begin to slide onto my backside once again.

"Hey," a menacingly deep voice barks from behind, and I turn to find a tall, dark, and broodingly handsome man—and lucky for me, he happens to be my husband.

Jasper is bearing a plastic sword in his hand, and the way he was brandishing it you'd think he was about to cut someone with it—and that someone would be Griffin.

"Hello, Dizzy." A brunette crops up next to him dressed as Cleopatra, and I recognize the witch under all that dark kohl and red lipstick.

"Camila?" I step away from Griffin to examine the sight before me. "Wait a minute. Are the two of you dressed up as Cleopatra and Marc Antony?"

A smile slithers over Camila's lips. "Someone paid attention in history class." She nudges Jasper. "I told you everyone would know who we were." Her smile widens. "Jasper tried to put up a fight, but I looked the place up online and saw that costumes were highly recommended. Bizzy—I see you and your date have gone the extra mile, too."

"Matching hats?" Jasper looks disgruntled by the fact as he inspects the pink wonder sitting on my head.

"I wasn't as investigative as Camila," I say. "I came without a costume, and Griffin just so happened to have another hat handy."

"Hat trick." Griffin pretends to shoot Jasper, and Jasper looks as if he's about to reach for his gun.

Hat trick, huh? Jasper muses. *I bet that's just his first trick of the night. It looks as if I showed up just in time.* He nods my way. *Sorry about Camila. Once she heard where I was going, she followed me right over and thrust this sword into my hand. I won't lie. I'm wishing it were real. I've been to enough crime scenes to know I can stage one well enough to make it look like an accident.*

Good grief.

If Jasper knew half the things Griffin was thinking, he'd move that crime scene up on the agenda. Good thing I'm the only mind reader in the family.

Griffin pulls me close again and glues his pelvis to mine.

On second thought, Jasper doesn't need to be a mind reader to know any of Griffin's unchaste intentions.

"How about we have dinner?" I ask, attempting to push Griffin off of me.

"Sounds perfect." Jasper reels me his way. "I think we'll join you."

Griffin doesn't bother hiding his discontent. "That would be wonderful. I wouldn't have it any other way." *If the guy wants to see me snagging his wife from right under his nose, so be it.*

ADDISON MOORE & BELLAMY BLOOM

My jaw unhinges. "A table for four sounds perfect."

"So, who's your date?" Griffin has the cookies to ask Jasper as we make our way to the table by the bar.

"Camila Ryder." Camila is quick to thrust her hand his way. "You may have heard of me. I've got my own talk show on YouTube with close to a million subscribers. It's called *Gossip Gal*, and I have all the latest and greatest juiciest bits of choice news."

Griffin pulls out a seat for me, and Jasper begrudgingly does the same for Camila.

Why does it suddenly feel as if I'm on a double date with my husband—and I'm with the wrong plus one?

"I don't think I have heard of it," Griffin says as we all get settled. "But I'll be sure to look it up." *Doubtful, but it seemed the polite thing to say. If I didn't know better, I'd think she was throwing out the feelers. No way am I falling for that again. I may have been easily distracted back in the day, but now that I've got a second shot with Bizzy, I'm not letting it go.*

A second shot? I gape at Griffin. Boy, he really is delusional.

Jasper taps his knee to mine. *This guy honestly thinks he's got a chance, doesn't he?*

I'm not sure I should answer that. We've still got dinner to get through, and I haven't even tapped into Casper family drama just yet.

I give a noncommittal shrug toward my handsome hubby. No use in inciting a shootout—just yet. The shootout seems inevitable at this point.

"My treat," Griffin says as he looks to the three of us. "Order whatever you like. As the owner, it's my honor to make sure everyone at this table has an enjoyable and delicious night." *I'll have to keep reminding Bizzy that I own this joint. I like the idea of sweetening the pot. She could be living on Easy Street with me. We'll find someone else to run the inn. Maybe Camila could take over those duties as well as Bizzy's wifely duties with this gun-slinging goof.*

I make a face at the thought. As if I'd ever approve of her lifting a finger at my precious inn—or with my precious husband.

"I'm moonlighting at the inn now, too," Camilla says to Griffin. "I've been hired to act the part of a witch in their Halloween extravaganza.

"There's no acting involved," I say.

Griffin, Camila, and even Jasper lift a brow my way.

"What I mean is, it's just a haunted house. It's not a play." She made it sound like her Broadway debut was imminent. "Camila is one in a cast of thousands."

She glares over at me. "Yes, well, there's no part too big or small. I like to take a professional approach when it comes to my acting."

"I'm sure you'll be a natural," I mutter as I look down at the menu.

A waitress comes by, dressed as a skeleton with ghoulish bruises around her eyes, and takes our orders.

Both Jasper and I ask for the special—a burger with onion rings and fried okra. Griffin gets something called the king sausage, and Camila takes Griffin up on his offer and orders the most expensive item on the menu—a tower of crab legs.

Our orders say so much about our personalities, it's downright scary.

"So Griffin"—Jasper forces a smile—"tell me about Drive. It's one of three transportation apps in all of Maine. You must be doing well with that."

"One of three in the country," he corrects. His gaze slides

my way. *Once Bizzy realizes I'm swimming in it, she'll dump the cop right into the witch's lap. I can tell Camila would prefer to save a broom and ride this guy's sword instead, and I'm not talking about the plastic one he charged at me with.*

A choking sound comes from me just as a waiter dressed as a pirate lands a round of water onto the table.

"Wine, please." Griffin lifts a finger to the pirate. "The best we have in the house. These are my friends." The waiter nods and takes off just as Griffin offers me a toothy grin. "Yes, indeed, Drive is doing far better than I ever could have imagined. It's still a relatively new startup, but we've shattered all of our financial forecasts. We've already edged out one of our competitors, and we're just about to do the same for the other." He cast a glance toward Jasper. *Just the way I'm about to edge you out, buddy.* He winks his way.

Jasper growls, *This guy is a slime, Bizzy. Here's hoping he turns out to be the killer. I'd love to bash his head through a wall and leave the consequences at the door.*

"Jasper"—I gasp— "was Barnabas Casper's death ruled a homicide?"

Okay, so maybe I shouldn't have gone there just yet, but holding off for another second might have cost Griffin his gray matter. And I need his gray matter for at least another half hour.

Jasper's chest expands. "It was ruled a homicide." He gives a stern look to Griffin. "They found a compound called saxitoxin in his bloodstream. It was ingested via a cupcake he ate."

"Saxitoxin? What's that?" I ask.

"A paralytic found in shellfish after they ingest toxic algae blooms." Jasper nods. "At the right dose, it can be lethal."

Camila shudders. "I'm guessing the killer knew the right dose."

I shoot her a look that says stay out of my investigation.

Griffin shakes his head. "Murder?" He gives a long blink. "I hate to say it, but if anyone had the enemies to do something like that, it was Barn. Like I mentioned to you this morning, Bizzy, Sabrina had a bone to pick with him." *I can't believe I just threw that poor girl under the bus. Heaven knows she's been through enough. And to the lead homicide detective, no less?* He frowns over at Jasper. *I'd better defuse this bomb.*

"I ran into Sabrina Chambers at the Montgomerys' farm today," the words speed out of me in fear Griffin will turn the conversation around in order to help out his friend. "I went out to pick up some pumpkins." I decide to leave out the fact Georgie destroyed the barn yet again. "Sabrina mentioned that her dad and Barnabas' father had a falling-out. A very bad one."

Griffin winces. "Did she tell you how childish things got between them?"

I nod before looking to Jasper. "Barnabas' father—Barnabas Senior, caught his buddy having an affair. Threats were made. Mr. Chambers resorted to sophomoric tactics—evictions, spreading rumors at the office that the Caspers were squatters, other petty things that were pretty terrible."

He lifts a brow. "Do you think it's a motive for murder?"

"I don't know. But they dated." I bite down on my lip once I realize that I just expressed a thought Sabrina had.

"She told you that?" Griffin seems amused. "I thought for sure she had swept that under the proverbial rug."

Our food arrives, and Greta the angry cavewoman is one of the servers delivering the feast. Camila's ridiculously tall tower of crab legs is set in the center of the table, and now it looks as if our meager meal will struggle to find a home around it.

"One house special for you." She winks over at Jasper as she lands his plate before him. "And one for you, my love." She bares her fangs as she sets my burger down. *A little extra sauce for Griffin's new whore. Here's hoping they both get a communicable disease.*

I can't help but grimace at my food.

Is she the one who's going to give us the communicable disease? By way of her saliva?

"Thank you," I snarl the words out. "It looks delicious." And sadly, it does.

Greta snorts. "Oh, it will be. Let me know if you need anything else." She runs her finger over Jasper's shoulder. "Especially you, handsome." She takes off, and Griffin tracks her with a death glare in his eyes.

"This looks divine," Camila marvels at the leggy wonder before her. "Come on, Jasper. Let's dig in together like the old days."

"You bet," Jasper says as he reaches for a crab leg and I clear my throat.

Jasper gives me the side-eye. "On second thought, I think I'll stick to my burger."

"Good move," I whisper as I pick an onion ring off his plate. *On second thought*, I probably should have let him snag a leg or two seeing that I'm going to have to nibble off his meal. "So Griffin, do you think Sabrina could have had access to a toxin like that?"

He squints my way. *I need to deflect. There's no need to bury Sabrina right along with Barnabas.*

"I don't think so." He shakes his head emphatically.

Jasper drums his fingers impatiently against the table as he looks to Griffin. "Who do you think could have done something like this?"

I look to Griffin myself. "Sabrina mentioned something about a woman by the name of Carrie Hazelman—the deceased sister?" Okay, so Sabrina didn't mention her, but she mentioned something about the family so I think it's a fair springboard.

Camila cracks a crab leg in half. "Carrie Hazelman?" Her eyes double in size. "Oh, I can't wait to meet her." *And I will at that Red Riding Hood Society meet and greet.* "I follow her Insta Pictures account. That woman was born in the lap of luxury. I bet she was wrapped in an Hermes scarf when she was born, and they'll swaddle her in one the day she dies. She has an army of personal shoppers at home and abroad. She lives in a twenty-thousand square foot house that overlooks the bluffs, and she just came out with her own nail polish line—infused with gold dust." She frowns. "Of course, I can't afford a bottle on my salary." She sweeps her eyes to Jasper. "But if someone wanted to surprise me with a bottle for Christmas, I wouldn't be opposed to it."

"Fat chance," I whisper.

"I'll barter." She grabs ahold of Jasper's arm. "I'll bake you a tin of my famous shortbread cookies. Okay, fine. *Two* tins. You always did drive a hard bargain."

"Two tins?" Jasper licks his lips as if he's considering it.

Am I going to have to clear my throat again?

Griffin chuckles to himself. *I won't have to steal Bizzy from him. She's going to dump him before I get the chance.*

I'd like for Griffin to be wrong.

"No." Jasper shakes his head. "Sorry, Camila. The only woman I'm buying gold nail polish for is my wife." He picks up my hand and kisses the back of it, and I reward him by stealing another onion ring. "What's this about Carrie Hazelman?"

Griffin ticks his head to the side. "That was his half-sister. His mother had an affair with Barnabas' biological father while they were both married to other people. At first, she tried to pass him off as her husband's child—even named him after the guy, Barnabas. He's an attorney out in Connecticut. Anyway, the truth eventually came out about his paternity. Robert Hazelman, Barn's DNA donor, comes from old oil money. The guy had billions shooting out of every orifice. He passed away about two months ago. Last I heard, Barnabas was in the will and his half-siblings were trying to fight it. A judge has issued a moratorium on distribution until the lawsuits were settled."

"What lawsuits?" I ask.

Griffin takes a breath. *Here goes the bomb.* "Carrie and her siblings didn't think Barnabas should get a dime since he was born out of wedlock. As soon as the old man took a dirt nap, the lawsuits rolled out. Barnabas' attorney assured him that he wouldn't have a problem getting his hands on his fair share. He said the courts cared about blood more than they did about morals. The Hazelmans had an uphill fight and they knew it. The most vocal of the bunch was Carrie. Don't think for a minute she came out to Cider Cove to watch a bunch of zombies staggering down Main Street."

Camila leans in. "You think she came down to do him in?"

Griffin nods. "You said it." *Here's hoping Jasper is firmly on Carrie's trail. Sabrina deserves some peace in her life.*

I inch back. He's really invested in turning the spotlight away from Sabrina. I wonder why that is?

"Griffin"—I lean his way— "can I ask you a personal question?"

"Anything, shoot." *The more personal, the better.* His lips curve my way. *And I do plan on getting personal with Bizzy. I'd say we were off to a great start.*

"Do you have a history with Sabrina?" I give a little shrug. "She may have hinted at something of that nature." She didn't, but he has no reason to think I'd make something like that up.

He winces. "No, actually, we've been nothing but friends. Pretty good friends. When my ex and I hit the skids, Sabrina was a good ear to lean on. I'd hate to think she misconstrued that." *I know she didn't. But obviously, Bizzy misunderstood. I can't fault her. She always was a romantic at heart.*

There's that.

Camila cracks another leg, and this time bits of crab shell go flying like shrapnel. She pulls out a thick, red, freckled piece of crab meat in one smooth move and Jasper moans.

"That's a good one," he says.

Note to self: get this man a crab tower from the Country Cottage Café asap.

Camila looks over at Griffin. "So what connected you to the deceased?"

"He had his own software startup," Griffin says. "Mostly coding, nothing interesting. He helped when it came to the software I used for Drive. At the end of the day, we were friends. Good friends." He sighs as the smile slides off his face. *Barnabas was the best, and now he's dead. It's not fair. Death never is. Although Barnabas was warned it would happen, and yet he insisted on walking a thin line.*

Warned?

"Griffin, do you think Barnabas knew the killer was after him?"

He gives an emphatic nod. "Everyone knows Carrie wanted him dead. She said so every chance she got."

Camila nods right along with him. "She's mentioned it in a few of her social media posts as well."

Jasper and I exchange a glance.

Griffin blows out a breath. *Of course, Sabrina wanted him dead and buried for reasons of her own as well. Everyone knew that, too, but I'm willing to let sleeping dogs lie. If Jasper is as smart as he thinks he is, he'll figure it out on his own.*

Wow. Could that be the smoking gun? It sure sounds as if Griffin thinks Sabrina is the real culprit.

We wrap up our meal, and Griffin walks us out.

Camila blows Jasper a kiss. "I'll see you in the morning." She rattles the enormous doggie bag in her hand. "And don't worry. I'll bring these bad boys to the precinct and we'll make a nice lunch out of it."

She takes off and Griffin offers me a spontaneous hug, his arms riding up and down my back as if looking for his keys in my sweater.

"Bizzy Baker." He pulls back and looks into my eyes. "What was I thinking leaving you high and dry like that way back when?"

"You were thinking that Mackenzie Woods might actually put out."

He gives a mournful chuckle. "Sadly, I was right. But if I could go back, I'd tell my high school self that you would have been worth the wait." He looks back at Jasper. "You're a lucky man." *But your luck is about to run out, buddy.* "Goodnight." He brushes a light kiss to my cheek. "Have a safe drive back. I'm going to hang out here for a little bit longer." He winks and waves as he ducks back inside.

"I'm going to kill him eventually." Jasper sighs as if it were a given.

"If you knew his thoughts, you wouldn't give him a

reprieve. But never mind that. Let's talk about Barnabas' murder."

"Carrie Hazelman certainly has a motive—a rather vocal one at that."

I nod. "To the undiscerning eye, it would seem to be accurate. But Griffin spent a lot of time trying to figure out how to deflect the spotlight from Sabrina Chambers. He said that Sabrina wanted Barnabas dead and buried for reasons of her own."

Jasper glances back at the establishment. "What did you think when you spoke to Sabrina?"

"I thought her father had more of a reason to kill the father of the deceased than she had to kill Junior."

Jasper pulls me in. "Let's talk to Carrie and see where that leads. Now, all we have to do is track her down. Leave that to me, would you?" His lips twitch.

"I'd love to, but I've already got a head start in that department. She's a part of some Red Riding Hood Society that Macy has been sucked into—and apparently, she's extended the invite to Camila."

"What's that about?"

"All I know is *werewolves* are involved."

"Figures."

"You don't look thrilled."

"Sending my wife to the wolves? That never thrills me. Come on, let's get home. I'll try to impress you with my wild and wooly ways."

"Only after I impress you with the crab legs from the Country Cottage Café," I tell him.

"*Ooh*, you know the way to my heart."

"And apparently, Camila does, too."

"I vote we don't mention our exes for the rest of the night.

The rest of the night is about you and me. As it should be—we make quite the team." He lands a lingering kiss to my lips. "It's almost a full moon. Ten bucks says I can make you howl a little early."

A laugh trembles from me. "I dare you to try."

We head straight for *Spider* Cove and fill up on crab legs and spider web cupcakes before we head back to the cottage and howl to our heart's content.

Jasper shows me a wild and wooly good time all night long.

Whoever killed Barnabas Casper might be having a good time at the moment themselves, but that good time is about to run out.

With Jasper and me on the case, they don't stand a chance.

Jasper is right. We make quite the team.

CHAPTER 8

There is nothing as exhilarating as Main Street in the fall. Crisp breezes, orange and red leaves raining from the maple trees, the shops decorated to the hilt in harvest themes with pumpkins, scarecrows, and something a little more sinister for the upcoming spooky holiday, Halloween.

Look, Bizzy, I can fly! Sherlock barks as he scampers ahead, and I drop the leash so I don't fly with him.

Oh, you cannot fly, you speckled floof, Fish yowls. *You can hardly walk a straight line in that thing.*

The *thing* in question would be the red satin superhero cape he's donned today as a part of his costume. And Fish is right, poor Sherlock has tripped over his cape more than anything else.

I don't want to fly, Nutmeg chirps as she looks up at me with those big brown eyes of hers. *I like keeping my feet on the ground just fine. And I like my costume, too.*

"You are too cute for words, Nutmeg. You, too, Fish." I sink a quick kiss to my sweet kitty's nose.

Nutmeg has a couple of paperbacks stacked on her back and a sign that reads *mobile library.* Nessa made it for her, and I think it's adorable.

Fish is wearing an orange sweater in the shape of a pumpkin, and it's turned her into more of a little heater than she already is as I hold her.

Groups of young mothers with gaggles of children stride up and down Main Street this afternoon. My guess is, it's a field trip of some kind. A Halloween-inspired field trip considering the fact each of the adorable minions is in costume with a plastic pumpkin in hand. There are fairies, and superheroes—much like Sherlock—princesses, ninjas, aliens, and characters from every cartoon you can imagine. The mothers are dressed up, too, albeit on a far less grander scale, some as scarecrows, others as cats, and some with nothing more than a butterfly painted onto the side of their faces. And, of course, that giant pumpkin at the end of the street is being mobbed by the masses as people try their best to snap a picture with it.

"*Ohh,* I just thought of something," I say. "We'll have to come back with Jasper, in costume, of course, and we can all take a picture with that giant pumpkin. Hey? Maybe we can use it as our Christmas picture. Do you think that would be weird?"

Fish twitches her whiskers. *It's only weird if Sherlock makes that crazy face of his. I think he does that on purpose to ruin our pictures. He knows I hate to stand still and say cheese. It hurts my cheeks to smile that hard for so long.*

The crazy face in question is sort of an odd anomaly. When Sherlock is told to smile, one of his eyes grows wide, the other goes crooked, and his tongue hangs out the side of his mouth. He does look a bit crazy, but in a fun way. Mostly.

Here we are! Sherlock barks and jumps as he pauses in front of my mother's shop, Two Old Broads, and I can't help but note the word *broads* on the sign has been covered with a giant piece of butcher paper and it reads *witches* instead.

"Two Old Witches," I say as I read the new signage.

Fish brays out a laugh. *Do you think Aunt Macy had something to do with that?*

"No. Unfortunately, I think the witches themselves thought it was a good idea. And for their sake, I hope it was. They've had a rocky road with sales as of late."

The entire reason I came here was to speak with Macy about the Red Riding Hood Society. She let me know she was doing damage control at my mother's shop, so I gathered the pets and we came right down.

"Let's head in and see what this is all about."

It's warm inside, and the shop is empty save for a couple of customers. The shop in general holds an eclectic mix of products, but by and large they primarily sell wonky quilts in every shape and size. I head toward the back where my mother, Georgie, Juni, and Macy are congregating.

Mom, Georgie, and Juni are all decked out in their witchy

attire, complete with green faces, black tattered gowns, and black pointy hats. Macy, however, is dressed in a tight red dress with strappy black heels and looks like she's ready for a night on the town.

I wave hello, and the trio of witches all cackle out a rather frightening greeting of their own.

"What's going on?" I ask, while Sherlock takes Nutmeg and heads straight for Georgie as she produces a few strips of bacon from her witchy wardrobe. "And what are you supposed to be, Macy?"

"I'm a slut." She gives a Cheshire cat smile. "Some dare to dabble in fantasies, but I'd much rather keep my feet firmly in reality. What are you?"

"I'm a farm girl from Kansas getting ready to be blown into a whole new Technicolor world by way of a tornado," I say, giving my blue gingham dress a pinch.

Fish jumps out of my arms and onto the counter. *And she tried to shove me in that basket of hers. I said no thank you. I could see Sherlock getting ahold of it and locking me inside with the lid. I'm already down seven lives because of him. I can't risk another.*

I sigh as Candy, Macy's white fluffball, runs my way and I give her a little pat.

Sparkly shoes! Candy barks as she does her best to graze her teeth over my ruby slippers. *Bizzy, tell Macy to get a pair like this. I'd love to start my day off with a mouth full of glitter.*

I'm about to translate when Macy holds a hand up.

"Don't even think about it, Candy girl. I'm not buying a pair of red slippers just to have you eat them. She's been on a chewing spree when it comes to my shoes. I've had to put them all into bins that she can't break into. It's not like I have any cheap throwaways I can give her. Ooh"—she perks up—

"Bizzy, why don't you mine your closet and put a doggie bag together for Candy? We would both appreciate that."

I make a face. "I'll see what I can do." I nod to my mother. "So what's the emergency? Macy said there was something going on down here?"

"I'll tell you." Georgie wags a finger at me. "Preppy here wouldn't cast a spell to increase sales, and now they're down in the dumps and so are we."

"I'm never going to cast a spell." She swats Georgie. "And neither are you. The last thing we need is to call the spirits of darkness to us. This is all for fun."

Juni grunts, "We haven't made a single sale since we've donned these ridiculous dresses. I told you both we should have been cute witches. We look like a bunch of hags."

Macy shakes her head. "That's not the problem. I surveyed the women who wouldn't set foot in the store, and they all said the same thing."

"What's that?" Mom asks, looking as if she were ready to shake her oldest daughter.

Macy shrugs. "They said they don't like to mess around with the dark arts. There was no way any of them were going to set foot in here. Face it, you hexed yourself by changing the name and posing as vixens from hell. The people of *Spider* Cove, and the tourists that visit, have old-fashioned values. They're God-fearing people who want nothing to do with something the good Lord says to stay away from. Don't take their rejection too hard. They're just trying to do what the Good Book tells them to do."

Georgie grunts, "It's back to the drawing board, witches."

"You're right," Mom says, plucking off her black hat. "What do we do now?"

Juni lifts a finger. "A witch burning in front of the store."

"Great idea, kid," Georgie says. "I'll bring the wood, the gasoline, and the matches. Ree, you can play the part of the witch. It was nice knowing you. I'll make sure to pick out a picture from your youth for the funeral."

"Funerals are fun," Juni says. "I met my fourth husband that way."

She's right. Sherlock barks. *Funerals* are *fun. People hardly pay attention to the dessert table, and I can sneak in more than a few treats that way.*

Nutmeg barks as well. *How can we get to one of these funerals?*

Candy growls up at my mother. *First, we need to burn Grandma.*

Good grief. Fish casts a glance my way. *Do you see what I'm up against?*

"Do you see what I'm up against?" I ask, even though no one else in the room will have a clue as to why I said it.

Georgie dips her green hand into a giant bowl of candy. "And here I thought it was the candy corn scaring them off." She pops a handful of the fruity-looking candy kernels into her mouth.

Mom scoffs as she scoops up a handful as well. "No, that was Brennan's excuse for not coming out today." *Poor man is half-afraid someone else is bound to lose their life this month—and if I didn't know better, I'd think he thought it was him.*

Poor Brennan, indeed.

Juni shakes her head as she grabs a handful of the sugary treat. "You can't trust a man who doesn't like candy corn, Ree. You'd better dump him."

"I agree." Georgie nods. "And do it quick because I sense he's about to dump *you*."

"He is not," Mom says with a grimace. *Okay, so maybe the thought has crossed my mind. I've tried to comfort him and tell him that none of my children are secretly serial killers—but that only seemed to exacerbate his suspicions.* Her gaze swings my way, and I gasp.

"Brennan can't be serious," I say out loud.

It just so happens that the only person in this room without fur who knows about my supernatural ability to pry into the minds of others is Georgie.

Mom shrugs. "It's his prerogative to pick and choose the candy he likes." *I just wish he'd choose to go with the flow and stop worrying about dying a slow and painful death at the hands of my child. Besides, I'd like to think if Bizzy were to off the love of my life, she'd make it quick and painless.* She frowns my way. *Or in the least, she had better.*

"I'm sorry Brennan feels that way," I say to my mother. "But even though there's a killer on the loose, I'm positive what happened here the other day was a one-off. Whoever killed Barnabas Casper was after him and him only. Jasper just ruled it a homicide."

Mom shudders. "I swear, Bizzy. Sometimes I think you can read my mind. How did you know that Brennan was afraid of the killer?" *Good thing she can't read my mind, or she'd feel sick that Brennan was campaigning hard to have me move away with him so we can both be safe.*

My brows furrow at the thought. "It seems obvious. He's said a few things in the past and it all adds up." I sigh because I hate that both me and my rotten luck might have something to do with the fact my mother's relationship is in peril. I'd best change the subject. If I dwell on it too long, I might inadvertently point the Grim Reaper in Brennan's direction. "In other news, the haunted house at the inn just kicked off. We have a line going all the way down the street. It looks like it's going to be a huge hit."

Juni snorts. "And now she reveals the true nature of her visit—rubbing our nose in her good fortune while this place goes down the tubes."

Macy shakes her head. "I thought we raised you better than that." She winks my way. "But seeing that you're my sister, and you own that haunted inn, that means I get to cut to the front of the line. I'll stop by to have the underwear scared off of me after work." *And lucky for Jordy Crosby, he'll be there to witness the event. I've been meaning to sink my hooks into him.*

I make a face at her. I'd warn Jordy, but he's well aware of my sister's schemes, partially because they line up so well with his. Speaking of which...

"Macy, I need to know where I can find Carrie Hazelman. I need to ask her a few questions about her sibling's homicide."

"Why?" She narrows her eyes my way. "You're not going to accuse her of murder, are you? I just got in with the cool kids, Bizzy. I can't let you go ruining things for me."

"I'm not going to ruin anything, I promise." My lips crimp as a lie begins to bubble up from me—a rather necessary lie. And who knows? This lie might just pan out to be the truth. "Okay, fine. I happen to know this involves werewolves. And even though I've never told anyone this, I've had an obsession with the furry beasts ever since I was a kid."

"Really?" Mom wrinkles her forehead. "Is that why you were drawn to Jasper?"

I inch back. "What does Jasper have to do with werewolves?"

Fish titters. *He's a hairy beast, Bizzy. Everyone can see it but you.*

Georgie waves my mother off. "Forget about the kid. Now that we know those blood-red robes can lead to a paradise of the wild and wooly variety, I want in, too."

"I'm in," Juni says.

Mom tosses her hands in the air. "I'd best go to supervise. If both of my daughters are going to play with men who try to make them believe they're part wolf, I'd like to be able to identify the perpetrators before they bark up the wrong tree."

Georgie nudges my sister. "Where, when, and how many werewolves apiece?"

Macy sniffs. "Tonight in Glimmerspell. And from what I hear, it will be a virtual all-you-can-eat buffet of the furriest, sexiest men in the world." She scowls my way. "Don't make me regret bringing you."

"You won't." I nod.

We're going to Glimmerspell.

A chill rides up my spine at the thought.

I know for a fact Glimmerspell is home to the vampires, werewolves, and fae that live among us. I have a transmundane friend who lives there, and she told me as much. And as much as I'd love to have a reunion with her, I think I'd best focus my efforts solely on Carrie Hazelman for the night.

She was suing her half-brother, trying her best to hoist him as far away from their father's money as possible.

Did she hoist him off the planet as well?

That's to be seen.

And I have a feeling I'll get an eyeful of everything tonight.

October in Spider Cove is one thing. But October in Glimmerspell is quite another.

Here's hoping I don't get the underwear scared off of me.

And as much as I'd like to bring Jasper along in the event that happens, I have a feeling I'd best row this hairy, scary boat alone.

Glimmerspell, here we come.

CHAPTER 9

*G*limmerspell is a small cozy town located not too far from Cider Cove. A quaint town with cobbled streets, and a bookstore called the Haunted Book Barn that is rumored to be haunted—and I know for a fact it *is* because my friend Billie Buttonwood told me as much.

Billie just so happens to be transmundane like me. But unlike myself, she's not telesensual. Billie is a traveler—as in she can travel in and out of the time continuum.

I won't lie. I wouldn't be too thrilled if that was the supernatural ability the universe decided to give me. Reading minds is terrifying in its own right, let alone flying to and from different centuries.

According to Billie, she can't control where she ends up, when she leaves, or when she comes back. All she knows is that those time-traveling episodes are directly linked to her hot flashes. Not every hot flash, not every time, but there's been enough frequency for her to know she's got a bona fide problem on her hands.

Glimmerspell itself is inland, prone to have a dark cloud hanging over its head all year round, and for some reason it has attracted a few too many paranormal creatures for it to ever be normal. And the irony? It seems perfectly normal because ninety-nine percent of the world has no clue what really goes on in this sleepy town.

We cross the adorable covered bridge that leads into this perennially haunted town. Mom has volunteered to drive us all over in her minivan. I brought Fish, Sherlock, and Nutmeg along. And Macy brought Candy.

I wasn't going to bring any of the pets for the ride, but as soon as they got wind Candy was coming along, there was nearly a revolt.

Once Macy told us there was a meeting of this strange society being held in the woods, I was half-afraid I might lose the dogs. But Sherlock and Nutmeg promised to behave. And as much as I'm counting on that, their welfare rides on it.

Macy procured a few red robes for us all to wear from her source—whoever that may be—and one of the robes is for Camila Ryder, who, yes, is also crammed into this mobile sardine can with us.

"Okay, where to?" Mom shouts to the back where Macy sits between Camila and me.

Macy flicks on her phone and blinds us with the light illuminating from it.

"Make a left on Evergreen Road and follow it until it ends. That should lead us to the Nomadic Woods. My source says they stretch all the way to Canada. Apparently, the werewolf dens have claimed this land for themselves."

"Ooh." Camila's shoulders shimmy, and the whole van shimmies along with her. "Here's hoping a werewolf is willing to claim me."

Mom scoffs. "You girls do realize that these so-called werewolves are nothing but silly people playing dress-up."

Georgie grunts, "Says the silly person driving the car. Don't listen to her, girls. Werewolves are real."

"That's right." Juni is quick to agree with her mother. "Mama and I know firsthand. These boys are going to be rough, and rowdy, and they like to stay up all night."

Macy chortles. "Finally someone who can keep up with me."

Camila sighs. "I hope there's one that looks just like Jasper."

"There is," I tell her. "His name is Jasper, and he happens to belong to me." I frown down at my phone.

I didn't tell Jasper where we were going, but that man always seems to have a sixth sense when it comes to my whereabouts.

The darker and the creepier the landscape around us grows, the more I'm not opposed to Jasper tracking us down.

We finally make it to the Nomadic Woods. Mom parks along an entire gaggle of other cars, and we get out and inhale the crisp night air scented with pine and damp earth. The moon up above is in its waxing gibbous phase, on its way to increasing ever so slightly until there's a full moon—which is due on Halloween night. I couldn't think of a better time to have an entire tribe of lunatics on the loose.

"Put on your hoods," Macy instructs, and we do just that. "Now follow me to the den."

The den? Sherlock gives a soft woof.

Fish mewls, *It's where they put bad dogs.*

"Oh stop." I nip at her ear with a kiss. "Sherlock, Nutmeg, and Candy, you be sure to stay close," I whisper as we trail behind our small crowd and into a darkness so thick you can feel it. There are just a few freckles of moonlight that have traversed the branches of the pines to dapple the ground. And Macy told us that under no circumstances were we to use our cell phones. Apparently, they can spook the werewolves.

We walk about six yards before Sherlock stops cold, causing the other two dogs to do the same.

Did you hear that? Sherlock vocalizes something just short of a bark.

I sure did, Nutmeg growls. *It's that striped creature right over there.* She points left with her nose, and Candy waddles up and strains to look in that direction.

Racoon! Candy barks, and without warning all three dogs dart off into the dark.

"Get back here," I shout, only to have Macy and therefore everyone else shushing me into submission.

Fish yodels, *Oh, for goodness' sake. I'll gather all three of them and bring them back. Don't worry, Bizzy. I can sniff you out in a crowd, and I have excellent night vision. I'll be back with those furry goofs.* She leaps from my arms and scampers off herself.

She could sniff me out in a crowd?

What's that supposed to mean?

I don't wear perfume. And my deodorant is non-scented. I'm seriously going to have to revisit that moratorium on scented lotions.

I trudge along until Macy lands us all in a clearing, where to our delight—and slight horror—we find dozens of women in red robes just like the ones we've worn.

How am I supposed to find Carrie Hazelman in this mess? Everyone is dressed identically, and with their hoods pulled over their heads, everyone's face is covered with shadows.

A sharp whistle comes from the middle of the melee, and we look to see a woman waving something that looks like a silver flag.

"Gather, my fellow lycanthrope lovers," she howls.

"Lycanthrope?" Georgie sniffs the air as if trying to decode the message via her nostrils.

The woman laughs as we form an intimate circle, standing shoulder to shoulder. I'm guessing this isn't the first red-robed rodeo for most of these women.

"Yes, lycanthrope," the woman enunciates. "It's a word with mythological associations that signifies werewolves. She backs up until she's standing in the middle of the circle and the moon shines over her like a spotlight, washing her features with its pale blue illumination.

I suck in a quick breath.

I think that's her.

"For those of you who are new here tonight, welcome." She gives a light bow. "My name is Carrie. And per our custom to retain a certain level of anonymity, we simply go by our first names. Welcome new and old members to the Red Riding Hood Society, where our primary goal is to commune with the *were-*people among us. As many of you know, there are two governing dens among the were-people—Dagen and Broman. The Nomadic Woods is a sacred place, which both of those dens have claimed as their own. First, we'll start with the collective affirmations to let the werewolves among us know that we see their kind in a positive light. Then, we'll start in on our cleansing breathing, to rid ourselves of the world we come from and the negativity it breeds toward their kind. Finally, I'll say a few words, and then we'll close with the call of the wild. Need I remind you that the were-community has not always responded to our pleas to spend time with them. They can sense those insincere among us, and if there are any of you here who see this as a joke, or who have come with nefarious intent, I bid you to leave now. I didn't trek all the way out here in my best pair of Louboutins to be ghosted by an entire den of handsome creatures. I've got needs only the wildest among these woods can tame. And to quote my ten-year-old niece, 'I came to play.'"

A titter breaks out among the crowd as Macy yanks both my mother and me by the elbow.

"You negative ninnies better hightail it back to the van," she hisses. "I came to play myself. If the two of you botch this up, I might get kicked out of the coven right along with you."

"It's a society, not a coven," I hiss right back. "And I can't imagine why the werewolves among us would want to out themselves to humans."

Macy clucks her tongue. "It's October. Everyone knows that's their high-mating season. We're here to offer up our services."

Mom sucks in a hard breath. "Macy Ree Baker. Please tell me this isn't some weird cover for a glorified prostitution service for hairy men." *I'd hate to go home and tell Brennan he was right.*

The sound of gunfire goes off, and both Georgie and Juni let out a whoop while the rest of us gasps in terror.

We look to the center of the circle where the thunderclap came from, only to find Carrie with a weapon lifted to the sky.

"Relax, it's a blank," she tells us. "I guess you could say I have a flair for the dramatic."

"I'll say that for sure," Mom pants. *If I end up dead, or worse, then Brennan will really get to say I told you so—even if he is saying it to my grave.*

Wonderful.

And sadly, Jasper might be standing over my grave saying the very same thing.

"Let the affirmations begin," Carrie's voice echoes throughout the woods as a throng of voices rise all at once shouting praises to the werewolf community and those that support it.

It all feels so silly. Mom and I roll our eyes at one another as the women around us shout ever so loud.

Carrie fires that gun again, and the crowd conforms to silence once again.

"Now let's breathe, my sisters of the night. In through your nose, slowly, taking in the goodness that this night has to offer, and the goodness that the were-community has given us so freely. Out through your mouth, slow and easy. Again," she commands, and we follow her sage breathing advice three more times until I'm dizzy on my feet.

I never was good at heavy breathing.

"And finally," she calls out. "It's time for the chant to begin. Remember, low and slow—until we build to a powerful crescendo."

A whisper erupts among us, and I can faintly hear the words *I'm not afraid of the Big Bad Wolf.*

The chant grows in both sound and ferocity as the words speed up at an unimaginable pace, and soon the woods are alive and shaking as we shout.

"*I'm not afraid of the Big Bad Wolf,*" Carrie screams, leading the charge as the voices around us thunder in unison.

"*I'm not afraid of the Big Bad Wolf. I'm not afraid of the Big Bad Wolf. I'm not afraid of the Big Bad Wolf,*" we shout again and again until our voices rise to the stratosphere and come back to us as a dark echo. Once we hit our zenith and can't go any louder or faster, our chant comes to an abrupt stop and we hold our collective breaths. We don't move a muscle as our expectations rise higher than our voices ever could.

"I hear something," Carrie hisses. "Quiet. They're contemplating their arrival. I can feel it."

The sound of footsteps traipsing this way enlivens, and within moments Sherlock Bones, Nutmeg, and Candy are all herded into the center of our circle by none other than Fish.

"Oh, for crying out loud," Carrie grouses. "Who brought the dogs?"

"Don't worry," Mom whispers. "I'll cover for you both." She clears her throat. "My friend Georgie Conner did!"

Georgie proceeds to swat my mother as the crowd around us groans.

"Sneaky move, Preppy." Georgie sighs as the circle disbands and women break off into groups as lively conversations ignite all around us.

"Better luck next time," Carrie shouts. "Just to reiterate, no pets allowed. The were-community can be skittish about sharing the spotlight with other furry beasts. Next meeting is

Halloween night in the woods behind the gazebo in Spider Cove. Seven o'clock sharp. We wait for no one."

A dull groan breaks out before the conversations pick up again.

Camila jaunts over. "This is all your fault, Bizzy. And way to go, getting your mother to cast the blame on that poor woman. I'll make sure you're not at the next meeting. In fact, I'm going to out you to Carrie myself."

"No, don't do that." I scamper forward. "I'll go do it myself."

Macy sniffs. "We'd better go with her, Camila. My sister has more tricks up her sleeve than a magician." *Hey? If this werewolf thing doesn't work out, maybe I'll scout out a magician to make my own. The first thing I'll have him make disappear is my annoying little sister.*

"No," I tell them. Especially not after that remark. "Please, stay put. You'll ruin my investigation."

"Fine." Macy sighs, and a blue plume of fog emits from her mouth. "But we'll be near enough to hear everything. You're confessing your sins tonight, Bizzy Baker, or I'll dig through your closet myself and find those ruby slippers of yours to feed to Candy. You're the reason the entire lot of us has to go home without any wild werewolf lovin'."

I make a face at her. "It looks like I'll be the only one who gets some wild lovin' tonight because my name happens to be Bizzy Baker *Wilder*." I hitch my head toward Camila. "From her I expect it, but you, of all people, should know my name by now, Macy."

She rolls her eyes as she looks to Camila. "Is she always this acrimonious?"

"Always," Camila grunts.

I press my way past them and thread through the crowd

until I come upon a familiar blonde with her hood down, her eyes squinted as she looks to the woman before her, and a laugh in her throat as they part ways.

"Carrie?" I call out as I step in front of her and inadvertently block her path. Great. Now what? I haven't even thought about how I might broach Barnabas' death in the middle of the woods while wearing a ceremonial cape. "I wondered if..."

"Oh, don't worry about it." She plucks something from her pocket and holds up a pen. "What do you want me to sign?"

"Sign?"

Fish runs up and practically floats into my arms. *Just go with it, Bizzy. I'm getting tired of herding dogs. And to think people say herding cats is bad.*

"You can sign my hand." I hold it out to her. "I'll be sure to take a picture of it."

"I'll do you one better and take a picture with you as well."

She tickles my hand with her pen before we pose for a selfie together.

"You know, I think we've met before."

"For crying out loud." Macy hobbles her way over, as does Camila. "Hello, Carrie, how are you doing tonight?" *Carrie Hazelman is not only my best customer, she's the reason I have a roof over my head. That's exactly why I have to closely monitor this situation, if not control it.* "This is my sister, Bizzy. I believe the two of you spoke the other day in Spider Cove. She's investigating the murder of your brother. If you could just humor her and tell her a few odd facts—they don't even need to be true—I'll be sure to haul her out of here as soon as possible. And don't worry. I'll personally make sure she never comes back."

"Macy," I hiss, pulling her to the side.

Fish yowls at her, *Can't you control this woman, Bizzy? Why do we bring her along on these things? It's as if we can't seem to learn a simple lesson.*

She's not wrong.

Carrie backs up a notch as she takes a look at me.

"Now you've done it," Camila whispers. "Jasper is going to be furious that you botched up his case. He's going to throw both you and your cat out of that hovel you live in, and he's going to come crawling back to me. Thank you."

I glance to the sky while Fish growls.

He's not kicking us anywhere, Fish hisses in Camila's direction. *Set the witch straight, would you?*

I would, but a tiny part of me fears she might be right.

Carrie squints over at me. "Why are you investigating? Are you a detective? A reporter of some kind?"

"No," I'm quick to tell her. "I'm neither of those things. I own the Country Cottage Inn. Barnabas was actually thinking about doing some work on my computer systems." It's true for the most part. "But well, he never made it home from that zombie walk."

"Oh, he made it home, all right." Her cheek flickers. "In the spiritual sense."

Fish lands her paw on my chest. *Wasn't that glib of her? I think she did it, Bizzy.*

I would be so inclined to believe it, too. Her motive is money, and that's one of the biggest reasons in the book as far as murder goes. But Griffin was bent on protecting Sabrina. Why?

"Carrie, what do you know about Sabrina Chambers? She works over at the Montgomerys' farm. Have you met her before?"

Her lips purse. "Sabrina?" She casts a glance to the sky.

"I'm sorry. I didn't run in the same social circles as Barnabas. Actually, Barnabas and I weren't friends either. We were related—loosely. My father had him out of wedlock. At first, his mother, Brandi, tried to hide the paternity to save her marriage, but the lure of my father's billions was too tempting for her to resist. And, of course, once my father found out he had a male heir, he was delighted. But he didn't jump through the hoop that Brandi wanted—which was putting her son directly into the line of inheriting enough money to walk to the moon on. So Brandi and Barnabas teamed up and the wooing began. They fought hard to get their hands on my grandfather's inheritance—which trickled down to my father, tooth and nail."

"How did they do that?" Camila asks. *Don't worry, Dizzy. I'll help you steer this ship back to port. Why? Because I know you're too honest to take the credit if I garner all the clues. You'll practically be forced to sing my praises to Jasper.* A smile creeps up on her lips.

She might be right to an extent, but I don't plan on mentioning Camila to Jasper, ever.

Carrie huffs, "How didn't they do it? They took my father to lunch at least once a week—and they did it for years, all under the guise of Barnabas wanting to build a genuine relationship with him. The only thing Barnabas wanted to build a genuine relationship with was my father's money. And when my father died a few months back, Barnabas and Brandi must have really celebrated. Barnabas was in the will, all right—at an even split with my sisters and me."

Macy gasps. "The nerve." *I'd better let her know where my alliance lies, or I risk losing out on her monthly mega order.* "You know, Carrie, I sense this entire situation has emotionally drained you. I have just the candle to soothe your frazzled nerves—apple cider and pumpkin spice nights. I can have a dozen sent to your estate come morning."

"Send *two* dozen." She massages her temples. "Draining doesn't even begin to describe this."

A giddy scream goes off behind us. "I think we've got one!" someone shouts, and every woman in the woods runs in that direction.

"Let's go." Camila hooks an arm through Macy's. "We can take on all those women and hustle our way to the front."

"You're right," Macy hisses. "We'll hustle with the werewolf once we get to him."

Fish chitters as they take off. *I don't smell a werewolf, Bizzy. But I do smell a bear.*

A *bear*?

I'd better make this quick.

"Carrie, what do you think happened to Barnabas that day?"

Her lips twitch. "My mother spoke to the homicide detective in charge this morning, and he mentioned something about fish poison." She shudders. "We were all eating those cupcakes. I suppose he got a bad one. I bet something went terribly wrong in the kitchen where they were baking those things. If you do a little investigating, I bet you'll find out that they serve fish in the same place those came from."

I sigh. "I know they do," I say. "They were made in the kitchen of my own café. But I can assure you the neurotoxin that killed him won't be found there. That homicide detective happens to be my husband," I say softly. I'm not sure if it's the cover of darkness, or the fact I feel half-asleep, but I felt compelled to confess it. "Carrie, someone deliberately gave that toxin to Barnabas. It was no accident. Is there anything you can think of at all that can further this investigation?"

Good move, Bizzy, Fish says approvingly. *Now that you have her wheels turning, she may not confess with her lips, but her mind might just bury her with guilt.*

Here's hoping.

"You mentioned Sabrina Chambers." She shakes her head. "I think I have heard that name before. Chambers. I remember my father saying something about legal drama with Barnabas' father—his *real* father, not the biological one we shared."

"I heard about that as well. But that drama played out between their fathers. I don't know if it would be visceral enough to make Sabrina resort to murder."

"You're probably right. I certainly wanted him dead." *And I couldn't be happier that he landed on the other side of the veil. Both Barnabas and his mother were warts that landed on my father's will. The irony is that it was me who handed Barnabas the cupcake that night and shoved it in his face, but I'm not going to be confessing to that anytime soon. I value my freedom far too much. The last thing I want is a legal tussle to drain my father's fortune.*

I suppose those thoughts are incriminating enough. I certainly have to consider them.

She lifts her shoulders. "But just because I wanted him dead, doesn't mean I did it. Gentry James was there that night. He's a good friend of mine." She casts a dark glance to the woods. "Barnabas was doing some work for his restaurant."

A shrill scream erupts, followed by an entire cacophony of cries of terror.

"*Bear,*" someone shouts, and all-out chaos breaks loose.

Carrie disappears in the murky darkness, and I hold fish tightly as I do my best to spot those I came with.

"*Bizzy*," Mom screams, coming this way. "We need to get to the car, quick!"

"Sherlock and Nutmeg," I pant. "And Candy's out there, too!"

Within seconds, the sound of barking lights up the night, and we follow that vocal chaos until we come upon the trio of once-friendly canines bearing their fangs at a large lumbering beast that hobbles out of the woods and into the clearing.

"Oh, Bizzy," Mom's voice warbles. "I say we make a run for it, and you call the dogs once we're safely tucked in my van."

Do it, Bizzy*,** Fish yowls. ***It's called survival of the fittest for a reason.

"What about Georgie and Juni?" I cry. "And where are Macy and Camila?"

Camila? Fish muses. ***Really, Bizzy? Even faced with imminent death, you choose to be altruistic.***

"Who cares?" Mom grabs ahold of me just as the bear lumbers in our direction.

We're about to dart in the direction of the parking lot when Georgie and Juni step out of the woods, each holding something small, dark, and furry.

"Where did everyone go?" Georgie says, stepping this way. "Juni and I found our men. Would you look at these adorable little werewolves? They're playing coy, but I bet they can really show a girl a good time."

Mom gags on a river of words as she points to the tiny beasts.

And then it hits me. I know exactly what the two of them are cradling in their arms—and they're not werewolves.

"Those are *cubs*," I wail before I look back at the gigantic beast slowly moving in our direction. "And that's the mama bear!"

The woods light up with screams all over again.

Baby bears go flying.

I grab Nutmeg, Mom grabs Sherlock, and Macy reappears to snap up Candy—and we run like heck to my mother's minivan.

Mom drops her keys, and we all take turns screaming out expletives until she retrieves them and the entire lot of us jumps into the van—Camila included.

"Wait a minute," I say as I do a quick headcount of all the occupants—my mother, Juni, Macy, Camila, Sherlock, Nutmeg, Candy, and Fish. "Georgie is missing!"

Mom lays on the horn as we watch every last car around us speed out of the area.

Then out of the darkness, from the direction of the clearing, comes that enormous dark furry beast with a sole occupant riding on its back.

"This is where I get off, Toots." Georgie slides off the bear's side as she lands on the ground with a thud. "Don't let the little rascals get away with anything. And take some time for yourself once in a while. Believe me, there's nothing like a good, long nap." She strides our way, hops into the passenger's seat, and my mother floors it all the way back to *Spider* Cove.

I still don't know who killed Barnabas Casper. But I do know that Carrie admitted to shoving a cupcake into his face. And I think that cupcake just so happened to be laced with a lethal toxin.

She mentioned a man by the name of Gentry James. She said Barnabas was doing some work for his restaurant. I suppose he's my next mark.

Here's hoping he offers up some pertinent information that can lead to the killer, because I'm starting to run out of suspects.

There hasn't been a case that I haven't solved yet. But I suppose there's always a first time for everything.

But this won't be it.

Whoever killed Barnabas Casper is going to pay.

I'm going to track them down during this, the most frightening month of them all.

They may think they have nothing to fear, but they would be wrong.

A rather lengthy prison stay lurks around the corner for them.

And I'm going to do everything I can to escort them there myself.

CHAPTER 10

A bear.

"You met up with a *bear*?" Jasper sat wide-eyed with horror as I relayed every last detail of last night's fiasco over coffee, right here in our cozy little cottage. It's a small two-bedroom thumbprint of a home with a stone fireplace, yellow and white checkered sofas, and lots of pumpkins and maple leaf garland crowning every free space to remind us it's the spookiest season of them all.

I've always been a sucker for decorating for any holiday, let alone an entire season—thus the twinkle lights, fall leaf border, and mums and pumpkins set out on the front porch as well.

Jasper is already dressed for work, looking dapper in a suit, his hair still dewy from the shower, and his cologne clings to him like a dream.

I give a little shrug. "The good news is, we all came away with our limbs still attached."

"Always good news." He toasts me with his coffee. "Especially when my wife's limbs are involved. So I guess we need to track down Gentry James." He sets his coffee down and pulls out his phone. "Bizzy, promise me you won't talk to this man alone."

Fish mewls from the sofa in the living room, *Don't do it, Bizzy. Make no promises. It's easier that way when you're tempted to do whatever your free-thinking mind dictates. Tell him you'll think about it.*

I glance over at her. I certainly understand her concern. But I understand his, too.

"I promise."

Fish groans, *Next, he'll want to outfit you with a leash.*

I shake my head at the thought as I pull out my phone as well, but before I can type a single word into the search engine, Jasper flashes his screen my way.

"Gentry James is the owner of Wolfgang's Bistro," he says.

"Now there's a wolfie name if ever there was one. Maybe he's the real deal?"

"A werewolf?" Jasper's brows hike a notch before he reverts back to his phone. "The place is out in Glimmerspell."

"Ooh, now that just upped the odds of what could be hairy Gentry's DNA predicament. I love Glimmerspell. I can't wait for us to go. Hey? Why don't I ask Billie Buttonwood if she can join us for dinner? I bet she knows Gentry. It's a small blip of a town just like Cider Cove."

"Don't you mean *Spider* Cove?"

A laugh rumbles from me. "Don't tell my sister-in-law I slipped up. I don't want any part of her ire."

His cheek flickers. "Have you talked to Hux? I'm half-tempted to do a wellness check on the poor guy myself."

"Not a bad idea," I say. "I think he would appreciate it from either of us." I send Billie a quick text asking if she knows Gentry and explain the fact that I need to speak with him regarding a recent homicide. She texts right back. "Ha! Billie said she does know Gentry, that they're good friends, and she even invited us to dinner at the bistro to speak with him tonight at seven."

"Say yes." He picks up my hand and kisses the back of it. "Consider it a working date."

I text her right back before sliding my phone to the side and wrapping my arms around my handsome hubby.

"Any date with you, working or otherwise, is my dream date." I land a lingering kiss to his lips. "I can't wait."

"Me either." His lids hood low. "In fact, I have something special planned for dessert."

A guttural laugh pumps from me. "I'm already hungry for it."

AS SOON AS Jasper took off, I leashed Sherlock and Nutmeg and put Fish in a wonky quilt carrier strapped to my chest and we headed for Main Street.

The air is chilly, and the clouds above hang low with a

deep tint of purple to them. It's a perfect fall morning with orange, yellow, and red leaves raining down from the trees as we walk the cobbled path to my mother's shop.

I stopped by the Country Cottage Café and picked up a box full of Emmie's spider web cupcakes to share with the ladies. I had to come down and see if any of them came away with bumps and bruises after last night's dalliance with death in the woods.

Sherlock barks as he points his nose across the street. *Look at the skeletons in front of Aunt Macy's shop.*

Nutmeg yips that way as well. *They look happy.*

They should, Fish quips. *One of them is holding a whiskey bottle in their dead hand.*

It's true. Macy has quite the display in front of Lather and Light. A table is set out with a couple of skeletons seated at it. One dressed as a woman with a pink fuzzy scarf and the other dressed as a man with a tie and top hat. The man wields an empty bottle marked *whiskey,* and the woman holds an elegant teacup in her hand. Between them sits a basketful of three-wick candles with a sign that reads *skull smashing deal! Buy two, get one free! All fall scents are on sale today!*

I make a face at it. I happen to know that Macy marks up the candles so much that she makes a nice profit from all three. I can't fault her for it. The customers feel good about getting a deal, and she feels good because she can pay her rent.

"Maybe we'll hop over later and pick up a few candles? I owe Emmie for baking the best cupcakes ever, and the cottage could use a few new fall scents."

Careful. Fish lashes me with her tail. *Remember what happened to the cinnamon roll scented candle you bought? Sherlock managed to wrangle it from the glass container and gobbled it down in one big bite.*

"That's right." I cringe. "I'll be sure to put these out of reach."

It wasn't my fault, Bizzy. Sherlock sniffs my way. *I bumped into the coffee table and it fell onto the floor. The candle popped right out of the glass and I thought it was a treat. It wasn't all that bad. And Jasper said he didn't mind picking up after me in the yard because it smelled like fresh-baked cinnamon rolls.*

"That it did." I shake my head at the memory. And neither Jasper nor I have had a craving for cinnamon rolls since.

Nutmeg gives a few riotous barks as a group of six nuns storm out of my mother's shop.

"It's heresy, I tell you," one stammers.

"Justice will be served by a higher court," another says as the entire lot of them jaywalks across the street and straight into my sister's shop.

"What in the heck could have offended them so badly?" I glance up at the sign above my mother's shop and that butcher paper is back. But instead of reading *Two Old Broads*, or *Two Old Witches*, it reads *Two Old* Nuns.

"Uh-oh. I sense a little unholy disorder," I say as I open one of the bright red doors and the four of us file inside. The shop is light and bright; the scent of a pumpkin spiced candle warms the air. A smattering of customers mill around, tugging at the fall-themed wonky quilts with patterns of pumpkins, candy corn, and scarecrows all over them.

Sherlock and Nutmeg run ahead to the counter, then come right back laughing like a couple of hyenas.

It's hysterical, Bizzy! Sherlock barks.

Nutmeg gives a sideways jump. *I don't know what's so funny, but your mother just whispered that she'd give us twice the bacon Georgie offers if we can get you to turn around.*

Fish chortles as she spikes up in her carrier. ***Now, this I've got to see.***

She uses my chest as a springboard and takes off for the back of the store where I see Mom, Juni, and Georgie all huddled in a dark blob.

Now this *I've* got to see. If my mother is resorting to bribing my pets with bacon to get rid of me, something must be very, *very* wrong.

I take off the wonky quilt carrier and speed my way to the front just as the trio of darkness turns around.

Georgie, Juni, and my mother are all dressed as nuns—very pregnant nuns.

"Oh, for goodness' sake." I laugh. "That's what had those women up in arms?"

Mom grunts, "If by those women, you mean the six nuns that just stormed out of here, you'd be right."

Juni takes the pink box of confections from me. "They threatened to put a hex on us."

Georgie waves her off as she dives into the box of cupcakes. "They said they were suing us."

"They were not suing us," Mom says, snapping up a cupcake of her own. "They said they were taking the matter to a higher court." She takes a bite out of her cupcake while looking at Georgie. "I'd watch out for lightning bolts if I were you." Her shoulders sag. "That goes for you and me, too, Juni." She gives Fish a quick scratch before sighing.

"I don't know what their problem was," Georgie says while grabbing yet another cupcake. "I tried to tell them I was the fun sister."

"Yeah," Mom huffs. "I think the problem is that you're *too* much fun." She twitches her lips. "You know what? I think maybe we swung the pendulum too far in the other direction.

People have been giving us the evil eye all morning. I vote we change the name back to plain ol' Two Old Broads and just put on silly—non-offensive Halloween costumes."

"Good thinking, Toots." Georgie comes shy of winking. "I'll dress up as a platter of whale sushi, and I can lend the two of you a couple of mink coats. You can be socialites."

Mom snorts. "That won't offend anyone at all." She rolls her eyes. "No, thank you. We don't need a plethora of animal rights activists painting us in a bad light." She picks up Fish. "We're animal lovers, in the event you didn't get the memo."

"Are you kidding?" Georgie digs into the pocket of the black robe she's wearing, and her bulging belly shifts to the left. "I wrote that memo." She plucks out a handful of bacon, and both Sherlock and Nutmeg gobble it up as fast as they can.

"Save some bacon for me, Mama," Juni says as she drifts off to help a customer at the register.

"Get your own bacon, sis." Georgie empties out both of her pockets, and the dogs dance a little jig before polishing that off as well.

"She sure is cute." Mom gives a wistful shake of her head as she looks at Nutmeg. What are you going to do with her?"

"I thought I'd give it some time and see if any of the victim's family members or friends would claim her. If not, I've got me a cute little golden."

"She's as cute as a muffin," Mom says. "I'm hoping she ends up sticking around. Just like I'm hoping my customers will stick around after this latest stunt." She lifts her robe and unleashes the beach ball from around her waist.

Both Sherlock and Nutmeg scamper after it and have a ball with it, quite literally.

"Have you thought about selling fall or Halloween-oriented items?" I ask.

"The fall print quilts are practically selling themselves." Mom nods. "But we need something more."

Georgie nods. "Something darker, creepier, something that makes every person who sets foot into this shop feel the need to sleep with the lights on."

Mom sighs. "This is a cute, cozy shop, Georgie. You make it sound like a visit to the cemetery on Halloween night."

"That's it!" Georgie snaps her fingers. "We'll sell custom gravestones!"

"No, thank you," Mom is quick to eschew Georgie's grave brainstorm. "Granite is heavy, expensive, and takes special equipment to etch into."

"I'm talking Styrofoam tombstones, the kind you see on people's lawns," Georgie insists. "I'll make one for you, and you can make one for me. It'll be fun. And once we put them out on display, I bet we'll sell hundreds of them. I bet every married woman in this place would love to have a custom tombstone for her hubby. And she'll proudly display it in their front yard, too—year-round."

"Hey"—Mom straightens—"I really like that idea. Here lies Georgie Conner. She might be dead and gone—but her stench lives on."

Georgie makes a face. "Here lies Ree Baker. She wouldn't keep quiet, and now she's met her maker."

The two of them howl with laughter.

I glance at my phone, and it's nearly noon.

"Well, it looks as if my wicked work is done here. Glad the two of you have another scheme cooking. And as much as I'd love to put in an order for a custom tombstone, I'd better get going. I still haven't walked through that haunted house over at the B&B."

Jasper and I meant to on opening night, but we got a little distracted and never made it past the bedroom. And I completely approve of the ways that man chooses to distract me.

"We'll put the word out for you," Mom says.

"Thank you," I tell her. "The line is already wrapping around the building, but I suppose the more the merrier—or *scarier* as it were."

I pick up Fish and call for Sherlock and Nutmeg as we head out the door.

No sooner do I step outside of the establishment and take in the cool pine scent of autumn than a hand clasps over my eyes from behind. Someone yanks me in, and my back falls against someone's chest.

"Bizzy Baker—consider yourself kidnapped."

CHAPTER 11

*K*idnapped.

Sherlock and Nutmeg bark and growl like mad, and Fish yowls and hisses as she claws her way onto the perpetrator. And the sound of husky laughter expels from behind as the hand lifts from my eyes.

I turn around to see Griffin Duncan doing his best to fend off his animal attackers.

"Down," I say to all of my furry protectors. "Griffin!" I

press my hand to my chest. "You got my heart beating right out of my chest."

He chuckles while looking dashing in a suit. "I've heard I have that effect on women. How about lunch? My treat for being so terrible to you—both in the past and just now."

I consider it a moment. He did know Barnabas pretty well.

"Under one condition," I say. "We discuss the case."

"You drive a hard bargain, Bizzy. I'll tell you whatever I can in hopes to help out."

"Perfect." I flash a grin his way. "There's a diner across the street. Will that work, or is that not fancy enough for you?"

He gives an easy laugh. "I'm still the simple guy you remember." He pulls me in and we head for the Cider Cove Diner where we opt to sit outside to accommodate the furry among us. Dozens of pumpkins stacked on and around a bale of hay surround us, and it feels like the perfect fall day.

Both Sherlock and Nutmeg settle around my feet as they take in their afternoon nap, and I set Fish down on the seat next to me, snug in her wonky quilt carrier. Her eyes are looking awfully heavy, but I can tell she's trying desperately to stay awake. Fish isn't one to miss out on the action.

Griffin and I each put in our orders—a grilled burger for him and grilled cheese and tomato soup for me.

"So tell me, Bizzy"—Griffin leans onto his elbows—"what are my odds in snatching you from that husband of yours?"

A robust laugh bursts from me. "Zero to none. I'm afraid Jasper has won me over, lock, stock, and barrel. Trust me, you wouldn't want to be stuck with me. I'm still a small-town girl with small-town dreams. But look at you—you're a real jet-setter. From what I hear, your company has just exploded."

He shrugs. "I did just find out that Drive has made the *Forbes* list this year."

"Wow!" I inch back in my seat. "That's incredible. Congratulations."

Don't fall for it, Bizzy, Fish mewls. *Even if it's true, he's just weaponizing his business in an effort to nab you for himself. I don't trust him. He's shifty.*

She might be right, but it's impressive nonetheless.

He leans in. "Thank you. Care to celebrate with me? Champagne?"

"Oh, I doubt this place has—"

He calls a waiter over with a flick of his finger, and before we know it, a bottle of bubbly is being cracked open and poured for the two of us.

"Well, I didn't see that coming." I laugh as we toast. "To your great success. May you exceed even your wildest dreams."

"And you as well," he says as we clink glasses and take a sip of the sparkling treat.

"I better watch out," I say, putting down my glass. "Champagne goes straight to my head." And exacerbates my little mind-reading quirk in the most hostile way possible. I go from hearing a handful of voices, to hearing everyone at once, and every voice sounds as if it's coming from an amplifier.

He chuckles. *Straight to her head? I'd like nothing more. But then again, I don't want our first time to be due to some drunken error laced with regret. Nope. I need Bizzy to want me. And seeing that I've never had a woman refuse me yet, I don't think I'll have to wait too long for that to happen.*

My mouth falls open.

Fish titters. *He's thinking racy thoughts, isn't he?*

Worse—I nod.

She rolls her little kitty eyes. *He's a cad who's trying to trap you. I'd walk away now if you knew what was good for you.*

Maybe so, but we still broached the subject of his deceased friend.

I clear my throat. "Any word on a memorial service for Barnabas?"

His shoulders slump for a moment. "None. In fact, his mother and stepfather don't plan on coming over from Connecticut until the beginning of next month. I think they've done a little service at their own church, family only. I let them know I'd arrange for something small here." A group of teenagers dressed as ghouls of every kind walks by and Griffin and I share a grimace. "You know, Barnabas loved Halloween. Maybe I should invite a few friends down here to Main Street that night. We can share a few memories."

"That sounds sweet. I'm sure he would have liked that." I pause a moment as the waitress sets down our food. "I had a chance to speak with Carrie."

"Carrie Hazelman?" *Is she seriously investigating this case?* He shakes his head. "Tell me you're not putting yourself in danger trying to track down the killer. This person is danger- ous, Bizzy."

"Now you sound like my husband."

"It's a start." He winks. *I give it six months before we're shopping for a wedding ring.*

Fish groans. *I can tell by that smarmy look in his eyes that he's imagining a future with you. Just dump your champagne in his face and let's get on with it.*

I bite down on a smile. I can't fault anyone for their thoughts, no matter how outlandish.

I shake my head. "I'm not investigating. My sister actually invited me to some hairy, scary society that she belongs to."

His brows hike. "The Red Riding Hood Society?"

"How do you know about it? From what I can tell, it has a strict women-only policy."

"My ex, Greta, wanted to get involved. I don't know whatever came of that, but she followed Carrie on all of her social media sites and it was hinted at a few times."

"Can I ask what happened between you and your ex?"

"Only if you take another sip of your champagne." He lifts his glass and touches it to mine once again. "Come on, we're supposed to be celebrating."

"Fine, but only because you're an old friend." I knock back half the glass, and he's quick to refill it.

Be mindful, Bizzy, Fish warns. *I can't carry you home and neither can those two bumps on a log we've dragged here with us.*

She has a point.

"We grew apart." He shrugs as he drains his glass as well. "Greta wanted things I couldn't give her—emotionally speaking. She was tired of evenings by the fire, long walks along the beach, and people-watching at the boardwalk."

"Ooh, that sounds lovely."

Fish mewls, *He's casting a spell, Bizzy. Whatever you do, don't look directly into his eyes.*

I make a face at her.

"I thought it was lovely, too," he says. "But Greta is into the nightlife, going out until all hours of the morning, throwing wild parties. We just weren't a fit in the end."

"I'm sorry. That had to be frustrating."

"It was and it wasn't." He sighs. "Now all that's left for me to do is find someone who appreciates a slower-paced life." He purses his lips. "What about you? It looks as if married life suits you."

"It does. And Jasper is so great. You should really get to

know him better. He's charming and funny, and he treats me like a princess."

"But that line of work of his..." He sucks in a quick breath between his teeth. "How does that sit with you?"

"I'll admit, I get a knot in my stomach whenever I think about him running after killers. But, I knew what I signed up for when we met. In fact, that's *how* we met—he was assigned to a homicide that took place at the inn."

"At the inn?" His eyes widen as he takes another sip of his champagne.

I nod and tell him all about the long string of homicides Cider Cove has been plagued with.

"Geez, Bizzy." His eyes narrow with horror. "I think we need to move you about as far away from this town as we can get you. How about a nice beach house in the Bahamas? I'll go with you to make sure you're safe. We'll leave Jasmine here to protect this dangerous town." He winks and chuckles.

"*Jasper*," I correct. "And I don't think he'd appreciate me running off on him."

"So you're a real sleuth, huh? Thinking about opening up your own detective agency?"

"Me?" I laugh at the thought. "Never. If I never saw another dead body, it would be soon enough. But unfortunately, I saw Barnabas that day. Carrie mentioned that she fed him the cupcake. And that's exactly how the killer got the toxin in his system." I'll have to ask Jasper to be sure.

"She fed him a poisoned cupcake?" He quirks a brow. "Bingo. Sounds as if you found your killer."

"I can't be sure. I mean, her motive is pretty cut and dry."

He nods. "Rumor has it, the champagne hasn't stopped flowing at the Hazelman residence ever since Barn passed away. Carrie and her sisters didn't want to split their billions with anyone. Heck, they hardly want to split it amongst themselves."

"That's too bad."

He nods. "And the irony is, Barnabas was thriving without the money. He dubbed himself the digital king and had a couple dozen companies he was working with. He designed the software for the Drive systems and even added a few custom features that I wanted to input. Barnabas Casper is the only reason I am a very, very rich man." He lifts his glass to me and we toast once again. "Without him, I'd be stuck at Lucky Thirteen washing dishes right next to my ex."

Fish groans. *Please, I doubt he's washed a dish in his life. He's trying to look humble in your eyes. Now splash him in the face with your drink, Bizzy. Oh heck, smash him over the head with the entire bottle.*

I shake my head over at her before looking over at Griffin. "Well, I'm glad you met Barnabas. It sounds like you were really good friends."

"He was my best friend." *He knew all of my secrets.* He sighs. "I trusted the guy with my life." He leans in. "He was the friend I turned to when Greta and I hit the skids. We went big game fishing a few times and even hit the slopes. He used to tell me I was the brother he never had. And I felt the same despite the fact I've got three brothers. I trusted him more than I trusted my brothers, too. Anyway, he had sisters. Half-sisters via the Hazelmans and look what's become of him because of it?"

"You really think Carrie did it?"

"Don't you?" He tips his head my way. "The woman is diabolical. She was born with a silver spoon in her mouth. There hasn't been a moment in life she hasn't gotten her way.

And she made no secret about the fact she didn't want Barnabas to get a dime of her father's billions."

"I know. It all adds up, it really does. But she was in litigation. Why poison him? And with such a sophisticated modality. And how would she get her hands on a neurotoxin like that?"

He leans back in his seat. "One of her sisters does research for a marine biology firm out on Bass Island. Maybe that was the connection?"

"Bass Island?" That's just a ferry ride from here. "If you don't mind, I'll pass that on to Jasper."

"Not at all. I'd do anything to help track down the killer." He leans forward and takes up my hand. "This killer is dangerous, Bizzy. Trust me. The person who killed Barnabas doesn't plan on getting caught." *Thankfully, she hasn't mentioned a word about Sabrina. It looks as if that poor girl is in the clear. I couldn't care less if Carrie took the fall. Sabrina has been through hell. She didn't ask for anything that happened to her.*

He still thinks Sabrina did this.

I shake my head in disbelief.

Well then, I guess I have two bits of information to pass on to Jasper.

We finish up and Griffin walks me back to the inn.

He gives me a heartfelt hug before we part ways.

"Promise me you won't put yourself in danger," he says as he pulls back. "That's your husband's job, remember? He's paid to put himself on the line. You're paid to smile at your guests, just the way you're doing now."

A laugh bounces through me. "I promise."

I wave as we split ways and I head for the inn with Sherlock, Nutmeg, and Fish underfoot.

I'll do my best to stay away from danger, but danger seems to follow me like a dark cloud overhead.

I have a feeling Sabrina Chambers had better watch out—but it won't be danger tracking her down—it might just be justice.

CHAPTER 12

*J*asper and I dress to the nines, him in a dark inky suit and me in a purple number that hugs my curves like a racecar at the track.

It's date night, and we both happen to take it seriously—but not too seriously. We are, after all, tossing in a homicide investigation to keep things interesting. And for the past few years I've known Jasper, they have been serious indeed.

"Glimmerspell," Jasper says as we drive through the

covered bridge and we're instantly engulfed with darkness, nothing but our headlights to show the way out.

"Honk the horn," I say, reaching over and giving it a quick toot. Jasper gives it a few quick honks, too.

"That's what I love about you, Bizzy. You don't take life too seriously."

"And that's what I love about you—you don't either. You couldn't. You're married to a mind reader. Most men would run for the hills. And the fact you're currently in a town that's known for vampires, werewolves, and fae? It shows you like to live on the wild side."

"You don't really believe in that stuff, do you?"

"Why not? It's just a leap away from the transmundane. By the way, don't forget, if Billie up and leaves, it's not because she's trying to be rude. She might be having one of her traveling spells."

"Time travel." He shudders. "I worry enough about keeping you safe in the present. I'd lose my mind if you were whisked off to who knows where."

"Yeah, well, she only gets them when she has a hot flash. Here's hoping that affliction doesn't hit me once I get to midlife."

The car swerves slightly. "Please tell me there's not a remote possibility of that happening. I'll be gray by morning if I think my wife might blip out of existence. That's tantamount to being kidnapped by time."

"I meant the hot flashes." I chuckle. "Oh, I almost forgot. I was kidnapped today—by Griffin." I quickly fill him in on the incident, the lunch date, and what he said—or *thought*, rather —about protecting Sabrina. "Oh, and he said Carrie might have had access to the toxin that killed Barnabas because her sister works at some marine center on Bass Island."

"Whoa, back to the kidnapping. This guy actually put his hand over your face? Where was Sherlock?"

"He was there. And you would have been proud. All three of them went after Griffin."

"Can Griffin still walk?"

"Yes, why?"

"That means they didn't go after him hard enough."

A laugh strums through me just as we hit an adorable cobbled street. "Look at that." I point to the right at a cute little restaurant called Fae Gardens, adorned to look like a fairy garden with large metal flowers and butterflies adhered to the stonework on the exterior wall. "That's where I met with a suspect a few months back. It looks like a lush garden inside. There's a waterfall, and all of the waitresses have sparkly skin with tiny little wings on their backs as if they were real fairies." I bring my fingers to my lips. "Come to think of it, they probably were." The place across the street catches my eye. "Ha! Look at that. Rex's Stake House. *Good to the last bite! Blood bank bar inside.* There's even a cute cartoon vampire on the window with blood dripping down his fangs."

The streets are lined with twinkle lights up above, and each shop is decorated to the hilt with pumpkins, fall wreaths, and cutouts of ghosts, goblins—and an abundance of were-wolves, vampires, and fae.

"We're here." Jasper nods to my left as he glides into a parking spot.

"Wolfgang's Bistro," I read as I get out of the car. "Not a fly-by-night joint." I chuckle and Jasper does, too.

"That's a dig at the pointy-toothed among them, I'm guessing. It's all in fun."

"It's going to take a lot of convincing to get you to be a believer, I take it."

"I can't help it," he says as he takes up my hand and kisses the back of it. "I'm a hardboiled detective. I deal in facts." He presses those pale gray eyes to mine. "You're the exception to the rule. I believe and love everything about you."

I hike up on my toes and seal a kiss. "Thank you."

"You're welcome. You're supernaturally beautiful, inside and out. What's not to love?" He returns a quick kiss. "Now let's get the dinner show on the road."

"Someone sounds hungry for dessert."

"Why, I think you just read my mind."

We share a laugh as we head inside the establishment, and immediately our senses are overloaded with the heady scent of something grilled. It's dark, cave-like, lots of rocks on the walls, dark wood floors, and the music is loud and raucous.

A blonde waitress greets us dressed in a tiny red bustier and a tiny green frilly skirt. Her nametag is in the shape of a werewolf and reads MOLLY. I'm about to ask her what that delicious scent is when a waiter strides by with a sizzling cast iron pan of fajitas.

"That's what I'm having," Jasper and I say at the very same time and the woman laughs. "Let's get you seated."

"We're meeting up with friends," I tell her. "Billie Buttonwood and Gentry James."

"You're in luck," she says. *And if I'm in luck, this handsome man will turn out to be her brother.*

You wish, lady.

I quickly take up Jasper's hand and she frowns.

"Follow me." She sighs. *I knew it was too good to be true. Here's hoping Elliot dumps Billie. I wouldn't mind if that bad boy took a bite out of me.*

My mouth rounds out.

I'll have to give Billie the heads-up. We thread our way

through a sea of tables, and before I know it, I spot an all too familiar brunette with lavender-blue eyes.

Billie jumps to her feet, and I clamp onto her with a hearty embrace. We scream like a couple of long-lost sorority sisters while enjoying our reunion. In truth, I've only met Billie once in person when her niece brought her down to Cider Cove. She had just discovered her time-traveling quirk, and I was able to tell her all about the transmundane community. But we've been texting and emailing one another almost daily ever since, so it really does feel like I'm seeing a long-lost friend.

"Billie, this is my husband, Jasper," I say, pulling my hubby alongside me.

"So nice to meet you." A warm smile graces her face as she shakes his hand. Her dark hair is medium length, her eyes crinkle in the corners as if they were smiling all on their own, and she's donned an orange plaid dress with tall suede boots—looking ever so much the fall fashion plate.

It's only then I notice a couple of men standing next to her, both tall, both with dark hair. One looks far scruffier than the other.

"Bizzy, Jasper"—she points to the scruffier of the two with a dark brown dress shirt and a gold chain around his neck— "this is Gentry James. He's the owner here at Wolfgang's Bistro." She winces. "I hope you don't mind, I let him know you wanted to talk about the case."

"I don't mind at all," I say, extending a hand his way and he shakes both my hand and Jasper's.

"I'm anxious to help out any way I can," Gentry says. His eyes are a dark shade of amber that I haven't seen before. He has a wild and wooly look to him, and yet there's something undeniably playful about him. "The poor kid didn't deserve to go out that way."

"I agree," I tell him.

"And this is Detective Elliot Greenly." Billie waves to the other man by her side, who happens to be tall, dark, and broodingly handsome. If Macy were here, she'd make an obvious play for either one of these men. "My boyfriend."

My mouth falls open. "Billie! I'm so happy for you." I turn to Jasper. "Billie went through an awful divorce recently. If anyone deserves to be happy, it's her."

"I agree," Elliot says, and we share a warm laugh.

The five of us take a seat and quickly put in our orders. My mouth is already watering just thinking of those fajitas. I got shrimp and Jasper ordered beef, and we intend to share them both.

"So"—Billie wrinkles her nose—"don't hate me, Bizzy. I should have asked you first, but I may have shared your supernatural gift with both Gentry and Elliot."

"Oh no, it's fine," I tell her before blinking over at Gentry and Elliot. "I'm usually pretty tight-lipped about it, but with Billie, well, she's like my sister."

"They know about my little quirk, too." She nods. "And you've told me that your husband knows."

"It's true," Jasper says. "And we hope you don't mind, but Bizzy told me about your troubles as well."

"Gift," I say sweetly to Billie.

She shakes her head. "He had it right—*troubles*. I'd give an eyetooth if I could trade my traveling ways so I could read a mind or two. Anyway, I'm stuck with it. Just like I'm stuck with these two." She clasps onto both men beside her. "Gentry is our good friend. You can trust both of these men, Bizzy. We don't have any secrets from one another." She bites down on her lip. "In fact, we're going to tell you another secret because we think it might be pertinent to the case."

Jasper and I perk up.

"It concerns Gentry," Elliot volunteers. His dark brows pinch in the middle as if he weren't exactly looking forward to this. "And it concerns the deceased as well." He nods to Jasper. "I work for the homicide division in Winchester County. After Billie told me about the case, we spoke with Gentry. He shared a few details that we thought might be important. And for that to happen…" He nods to Gentry.

"I need to tell you my secret." Gentry grimaces a moment, and comma-like dimples dig into either side of his furry face. "I'm a werewolf."

"A what?" Jasper leans in a notch.

"A werewolf." He shrugs. "You know, hairy, howl at the moon—looking like every woman's dream after midnight." He winks my way.

Elliot chuckles. "Check your ego, buddy."

"Wow," I say breathlessly. "I mean, Billie told me that Glimmerspell is practically crawling with werewolves, vampires, and fae, but I never thought I'd actually meet any."

"Me either." Jasper doesn't look impressed by Gentry's declaration.

"You're not a believer," Gentry says to him. "All right, I'll do a partial translation."

"A partial what?" Jasper tips his ear toward the man.

"I'm better at showing than I am telling." Gentry gives a knowing smile before leaning in and looking Jasper right in the eyes as his jaw begins to elongate, and his eyes sink in a notch and glow like burning coals, while that scuff on his face grows out as thick and bushy as Sherlock's fur.

"Holy—" Jasper inches back and so do I.

A couple of waitresses come by with our sizzling feasts, and Gentry's face casually goes back to its normal formation —or at least normal as far as I'm concerned.

Our dinners land before us, and yet Jasper and I can't take our eyes off the man who just made his face morph into a teddy bear.

"Believe me now?" He lifts a brow at Jasper.

"I"—Jasper pauses to expel a breath—"believe you." He frowns. "I'm not sure if I should console or congratulate you. It's an interesting thing. Are there many of you? Is this something you were born with?"

A low growl of a laugh comes from Gentry. "No, we're certainly not born into it. But for the most part, family converts their own. To become a werewolf, you need to be accepted by the pack—of which there are two core packs that rule the roost, Broman and Dagen. I belong to Broman. We tend to think of ourselves as slightly more civilized than Dagen. Nevertheless, to make the transition from human to werewolf, you need to be bitten by a pack member—under a full moon, at midnight." He shrugs. "The midnight thing is more or less ritualistic. It could take place at any time of day, but we like the drama. And once a werewolf's salvia mingles with the blood of the victim, a peculiar infection takes place and the transformation of molecules completes the process." He glances at Billie and Elliot. "It's not as messy as it would be for one to translate into a vampire. With the bloodsuckers among us, their venom has a high kill-to-survival ratio. It's a fifty-fifty chance that the person looking to become a vampire won't survive the effort."

"Really?" I muse. "Then there must not be many vampires."

Gentry shakes his head. "No such luck. From what I hear, they have a list a mile long with people all over the world bidding to become one of those dark-winged creatures."

Elliot's lips curve. "I've heard the same."

Jasper leans in. "Gentry, was Barnabas Casper vying to become—one of your kind?"

He gives a single nod. "He was. I initially met Barnabas when he came in to revamp the software we use here at the restaurant. He got to talking to a few of the people in town —mostly women, fae, and he was able to pry the truth out of them. Once he learned that werewolves roamed the place, he wanted in on it. He said he had a life-long obsession to become one of us—that he's been living his life as a werewolf regardless. That he was immersed in Lycaon culture."

Jasper nods toward Gentry. "And you said he seemed believable."

"He did." Gentry's voice grows rough. "But there was a little more to the story. I was in the middle of the approval process when I discovered that his half-sister, a woman by the name of Carrie Hazelman, heads up the Red Riding Hood Society." He glances my way. "A group of women who gather in a ritualistic manner in hopes to call out a group of werewolves to mingle with."

I nod. "I was at their last meeting. I went undercover to speak with Carrie. Much to the group's disappointment, there wasn't a single werewolf that showed."

"We showed," he says. "But there were a couple of dogs and my guys can get skittish. Dogs tend to attack our kind. We can't blame them. It's their built-in defense mechanism. But we don't want to get the reputation for being brutes against animals either, so we don't put ourselves in the position to have to stave off an attack."

"Sorry." I make a face. "The dogs were mine. If I knew, I certainly would have left them at home."

"Don't feel bad," he says. "It was a blessing in disguise. Turns out, there was a mama bear and a couple of cubs that showed. I, and a few of the other guys, kept an eye on your group just to make sure the bear didn't go on a rampage, but bears can be twice as aggressive to my kind as dogs. It would have been a bloodbath had those dogs not showed."

"In that case, I'll have to tell Sherlock and Nutmeg they saved the day."

Jasper nods. "We'll have to give them bacon for their heroic efforts."

"Of course," I say before looking to Gentry. "And my cat, Fish, was there, too. She's the one that herded them back into the clearing."

"Is she?" Gentry says, amused. "Well, she'll need the biggest reward. Two of my guys almost ate those dogs."

"Ate them?" Jasper and I say in unison.

Gentry chuckles. "Kidding." His cheeks twitch. "But let's just say it wouldn't have been pretty."

Good grief.

"Gentry"—I lean his way—"I think I saw you in Cider Cove the day Barnabas died."

"You did. I came to tell him that we wouldn't be going forward with the process. His half-sister was suing him. She didn't want to share her inheritance with him. And there might have been a chance he was doing it to get into her good graces. It turns out, she's the one with the werewolf obsession. He didn't take it so well."

"I'm sorry to hear it," I say. "But you're right, Carrie is obsessed. And she's not sorry he's dead." I tell them everything I know about Carrie, and about Sabrina.

"Sabrina Chambers." Gentry glances away a moment. "I heard him mention the name Chambers, but it wasn't Sabrina. It was Justin."

The name ricochets through my mind like a memory.

"Wait a minute." I pause, deep in thought. "The day Barnabas died, Griffin, a friend of mine, was speaking with Sabrina and me. He mentioned that Barnabas' death was tragic, that he was still so very young. And Sabrina said he was thirty—same age as Justin." I'd better fess up. "I may have heard some of those things by way of their thoughts. But nonetheless, she knew Justin."

"Same last name," Billie points out. "It could have been a husband or a brother."

Jasper pulls out his phone. "Justin Chambers. Found him." He flashes his phone at us. "Died at the party. An accident involving a pyrotechnic about a year ago. Tragic accident."

"That's terrible," I say before turning to Gentry. "What did Barnabas have to say about him?"

He scratches the scruff on his cheeks. "We were working in my back office one night. He was running through the software, revamping it for me, making it more efficient, and we got to talking about the people we've lost." He glances at Billie. "He mentioned something about seeing someone die. He was reduced to tears."

"I bet he was at the party," I say.

Gentry nods. "Must have been."

Jasper looks to Gentry. "Is there anything else you could think of that might lead to a break in the case?"

He glances to the bar. "When he was working on my systems, he mentioned he could increase the overall financial efficiency. When I quizzed him on it, I wasn't so keen on the plan. I like to keep my nose clean when it comes to my finances, so I declined the offer."

"Dicey dealings with the IRS?" Jasper asks.

"Could've been." Gentry nods as if he dodged a bullet—a silver IRS-laced bullet.

We finish up dinner, thank Gentry for our meals, and I hug Billie extra tight before we head out the door.

Jasper and I head back to Cider Cove, and all the way there we try to piece together the puzzle that is Barnabas Casper's life.

But as soon as we step back into that cottage, we push all thoughts of homicide out of our minds.

Sherlock, Nutmeg, and Fish are already snug in their beds, so Jasper and I traipse into our bedroom.

It's time for dessert.

CHAPTER 13

*C*onfession.

No matter how much I love fall, no matter how far I'm willing to go to satisfy my obsession with pumpkin spice lattes, pumpkin pie, candy apples, candy corn, or even a cup of hot apple cider—I'm not a fan of having the pants scared off of me.

Halloween is just a day away, and I've yet to set foot into this haunted house of horror taking up residence at the inn.

"Come on, Bizzy," Jordy chides while wearing a mask that depicts a fuzzy brown teddy bear with round ears, bulging red eyes, and yellow razor-sharp teeth three inches long. The rest of him is dressed as an innocuous teddy bear, save for the knife jetting out of his back. "You own this place, and you're the last person in Spider Cove to go through it."

Suffice it to say, the haunted house at the inn has become an overnight sensation. And judging by the crowds we've had pour through here in recent days, it does seem feasible that the entire town—the entire East Coast has passed through our little contribution to this season of terror.

I crane my neck past Jordy into the darkened ballroom. The glow of purple and cobalt lights flicker, the sound of moody scary music blasts through the speakers, featuring the sound of creaking doors, sodden footsteps, moaning, and blood-curdling screams every now and again. And that doesn't count for the fact the people who are willing to set foot into this nightmare are howling and screaming, too.

"It sounds as if you're butchering people alive," I point out as Grady collects twenty bucks apiece at the door while ushering in the nonstop stream of people.

"We are," Jordy says, tipping his teddy bear head to the left. "But that's not until the end. Look, here comes Emmie and Leo. They're just getting out of it."

Emmie and Leo stumble this way holding their stomachs while laughing.

Emmie is dressed as Cinderella, and Leo is in his tan deputy uniform, gun included.

"Oh, Bizzy." Emmie wipes the tears from her eyes. Her dark hair is in an updo, and her blue eyes match her taffeta dress. "You're going to love it. It's not scary at all."

"Says the woman who's been in it twice," I say.

Leo shakes his head. "This is our sixth time. Head on in, Biz. You'll have a blast."

"Easy for you to say," I tell him. "You went in with a weapon."

He chuckles as he pecks a kiss to Emmie's lips. "I'll see you later. I'd better get back to work. We'll head in again tonight."

"You bet." She touches his lip with her finger. *And that fantasy you had about the red room in there? I'll make sure it happens.* She winces as she looks my way. "Sorry." She wrinkles her nose. *That was meant for Leo.*

I give a curt nod. Emmie has a hard time remembering that I can read her mind as well.

I don't blame her. Half the conversations she has with Leo are telepathic these days, and most of those are steamy.

"I gotta run, too." Emmie pulls me into a quick embrace. "Nice costume, by the way." She irons out the front of my plain white gown with her hand. "Wow, Bizzy, are you wearing your wedding dress?"

"Yup. But I'm dressed as a Greek goddess. See?" I point out the giant gold cuffs on my arms and the gold wreath in my hair. My wedding dress had gold threading woven into the braided straps that crisscross over my back and through the gold belt that sits at its high empress waist.

Emmie cringes. "Is Jasper okay with you wearing your wedding dress as a Halloween costume?"

"I have no idea, he hasn't seen me yet. But I'm sure he'll be thrilled I'm not spending any more money at the Halloween shop. I've already worn just about everything I bought, except for the costume I'm wearing on the big wicked night. It was either this or I start recycling what I've got. I thought this would be fun. Besides, when am I ever going to wear this again?"

Emmie laughs. "You're so right. Plus, this way you'll get another wedding night out of it. I'll make up a giant bowl of clam chowder for you and Jasper and even throw in a few cupcakes for dessert. Think of it as a wedding gift."

She and Leo part ways with a wave just as Fish, Sherlock, and Nutmeg head this way.

Once they woke up this morning, I told them all about the fact they were heroes, according to Gentry, and all three of them have been adorably insufferable because of it.

They've all dressed up, too, of course. Since they're *unofficially* official employees of the inn, they dutifully each put on their Halloween costumes for the day.

Fish has a giant triangle lying over her back sprinkled with fake cheese and pepperoni as she parades around as a slice of pizza.

Nutmeg has a giant black spider over her back with four furry legs dangling off either side of her. It takes up her entire body, and there's even a giant red heart on the spider's behind signifying the fact she's the deadliest yet most loving spider there is—a black widow with heart.

Last but not least, Sherlock has a giant lion's mane enwreathing his head in a ball of fuzzy glory, and as a finishing touch we've attached a fuzzball of tan fur to the tip of his tail.

Jordy laughs at the sight of the three of them before scooping up Fish.

"I was wondering how I was going to cure the rumbling in my tummy." He pretends to take a bite out of her back and she playfully swats him.

Bizzy! Sherlock barks up at me. *I know what I want to be for the big Howl-o-ween parade tomorrow.*

Let me guess, Fish yowls. *A cat.*

149

Nutmeg brays out a laugh.

Why would I want to be a cat? Sherlock gruffs. *I want to be bacon. Everyone loves bacon.*

Oh, good grief, Fish yowls. *I hope someone eats you.*

"*Fish.*" A laugh bubbles from me as I give her a quick scratch.

Nutmeg yips and jumps. *I volunteer to eat Sherlock! Once he's a giant juicy chunk of bacon, of course.*

"What do you say, Bizzy?" Jordy asks. "Are you going in?"

"Are you going in with me?"

"He doesn't have to," a deep voice strums from behind, and I turn to find Griffin in jeans and a flannel. "Wow." His eyes ride up and down my body. *I'm going to have to make Bizzy Baker my bride if it's the last thing I do.* "You are a knockout. What do you say? You and me, and a certain haunted house? I'll let you hold my hand. I'm afraid of the dark." He winks.

Fish moans, *Can we turn him into bacon, too? Nutmeg, you'd have your fill of the stuff if I got my way.*

I'm going in with you, Sherlock growls over at Griffin. *Jasper said he doesn't trust the goof.*

Nutmeg barks right alongside him. *I'm going in, too. Sherlock might need me as backup.*

Fish gives a hearty sigh. *I suppose my paw has been forced.*

I scoop her up and shrug at Griffin. "Let's do it."

A greasy grin slides across his face. *Something tells me, it won't be the last time I hear those words.*

I frown up at him. Something tells me it will.

"Have fun, kids," Jordy says as he escorts us into the dark cave that was once my elegant ballroom.

A sign backlit by strobe lights reads *Welcome to Creepy Hollow.* It says something just below that, too, but I can't read it lest I risk having a seizure.

"How have I not been sued by now?"

Griffin laughs as he wraps an arm around me, and sadly, I don't protest.

"Let's plow through this thing," he says as he walks us into the entry, and soon we're transported into what looks like a forest with fake trees and blue ground fog floating around our ankles as purple lights vibrate in the background. The music tenses up, and every last one of my nerves is alive with terror.

Someone screams and I scream, too, in keeping with the vocal theme. A demonic clown jumps out from behind a tree, and the five of us bolt out of the room and onto the next.

Sherlock barks. *Don't worry, Bizzy. I'll protect you.*

Nutmeg shivers. *Would you protect me, too? I plan on closing my eyes until I get out of here.*

Fish meows as she burrows her face into my chest. *I'm one step ahead of you.*

Sherlock butts up against Nutmeg as if to lead the poor thing just as a white flashing light blinds us intermittently and an entire herd of zombies heads this way.

All of us scream and howl our way through the undead melee until we make it to the very next clearing.

"Geez," I shout, pressing a hand to my chest. "I might just sue myself."

Griffin holds me close. "I might encourage it—that is, if we make it out alive."

Next up is a room cordoned off with caution tape on either side of us and an entire gaggle of bloodied bodies lying in a heap.

"I bet they're going to jump to life," I shout up over the menacing organ music doing its best to destroy our eardrums.

The sound of a chainsaw enlivens before he can answer, and soon a madman in a hockey mask is chasing us from one end of the room to the other. He comes right at us and swings his chainsaw between Griffin and me and sends us darting in opposite directions.

"Whoa," Griffin shouts. *If I didn't know better, I'd think that was Bizzy's husband.*

The man in the hockey mask swings his weaponry rather violently toward Griffin's head, and for a second, I fear his theory might be right.

"I hate everything!" I scream as we make a mad dash for the exit and step into a veritable graveyard.

It's cool in this next installment of terror as tombstones peek out from the fog as we trek on by, and the trees in the background seem to be moving right along with us.

"This is too creepy," I whisper.

Fish pats me over the chest. *I'm thinking we should fire Jordy. Then set fire to the ballroom in general.*

"Not a bad idea," I say. "I'll get insurance money, and he'll get unemployment. There aren't any real losers."

Griffin wraps an arm around my waist and pulls me close. "Don't worry, this scene doesn't look that bad."

No sooner do the words leave his lips than an entire slew of hairy, scary monsters jump out from behind the tombstones, howling and clawing in our direction as they chase us right on out of there.

My voice rubs raw from all the screaming, and just when I think it can't get any worse—it gets worse by a haunted mile.

Ghosts—lots of them whistle around us, through us, and over us.

A part of me wants to inspect them and figure out how it's even possible to have a room full of poltergeists, and then another part of me fears this might be a room full of all the poor souls who lost their lives right here at the Country Cottage Inn.

Griffin and I howl our way from one chamber of terror to the next. The poor dogs are losing their minds, and their sense of direction—so Griffin and I each pick one up. He holds Sherlock, the bigger of the two. And I pick up Nutmeg. Fish has pretty much attached herself to my dress by way of her claws, so I don't have to worry about losing her.

We fumble and stumble through haunted forests, prison cells that happen to be aflame, and a butcher shop where indeed people are being sliced and diced in the most gruesome way—until finally we're spit back out into the safety of the inn proper.

Griffin has one arm around Sherlock and one arm still firmly around my waist as we pant and stagger our way to safety.

"Bizzy?" a familiar voice calls out, and I turn to find Jasper looking daring in a dark suit, his briefcase dangling from his hand.

A green-faced wicked witch stands next to him, gloating in her sexy little black dress and pointy hat.

"Well, well," Camila says. "What do we have here?"

"Yes." Jasper steps forward, his brows narrowing over us. "What do we have here?" He blinks over at me. "Bizzy, is that your wedding dress?"

Camila cackles. "Don't worry, Jasper. Once we marry, I'll have my wedding dress hermetically sealed, and nary a cat or an ex-boyfriend will be dangling from it." She straightens. "Wait a minute. If she's wearing her wedding dress as a Halloween costume, that must mean she sees you as some cheap accessory. Let's get out of here, Jasper. We'll leave the details of the divorce to her brother. I can have us on a cruise to the Caribbean in less than twenty-four hours."

Jasper blindly hands his briefcase to Camila while he stares Griffin down.

His jaw redefines itself. "Are you holding my wife and my dog?"

Griffin's chest bucks with amusement. "I guess I am."

Both Sherlock and Nutmeg scamper to the floor just as Jasper yanks Griffin away from me.

Jasper lands a right hook over the guy's face before I can protest.

"Jasper!" I scream just as Jordy speeds over and breaks it up before things can go any further. "Griffin, I'm so sorry."

"It's okay." He pats his lips with the back of his hand before inspecting it for blood. "I'd get a little heated, too, if another man was pawing at you." He stretches a short-lived smile to Jasper. "That is, if she were my wife." *And she will be.* "I'd better get some ice." He takes off in the direction of the café.

"Bravo, Bizzy." Camila gives a spontaneous applause. "You defended your ex and apologized for your husband's brutish behavior. How does that make you feel, Jasper?"

"Like I married a real lady." He offers a sheepish smile my way. "I was a brute, wasn't I?"

"If you knew half his thoughts, he wouldn't be alive." I pull Jasper in close and land a steamy kiss to his lips. "What are you doing home so early?"

Camila steps in. "Jasper was just about to escort me into the haunted house."

"To find you," he says. "I came home early because I wanted to show you something."

"All right," Jordy groans. "Let's keep it PG in the foyer."

"Speaking of PG," I say. "Jordy, that man with the chainsaw was way over the top."

"We don't have a man with a chainsaw."

"What?" I howl. "Gah!"

"Kidding." His chest bumps with a laugh. "Come on, Camila. You're late. And just for that, you'll be working with the man with the chainsaw."

"Ugh," she moans as she hands Jasper back his briefcase. "I hope he's cute under that mask."

They take off and I offer a sorrowful smile to my handsome husband. "Forgive me," I say as Fish curls back into my arms, a little worse for wear, her fur still on end. "I wish it were you who took me through that haunted horror."

"Wanna go back?"

Sherlock, Nutmeg, and Fish all bark and yowl respectively.

Jasper tips his head my way. "I take it that's a hard no?"

"A very hard no. Now, what did you want to show me?"

"Let's get back to the cottage. Like Jordy said, this show is PG."

"And the show that's about to take place at the cottage?"

"It's confidential. On a need-to-know basis." He pulls me in. "And you're going to want to know every last word."

WE HEAD BACK to the cottage, and I give fresh water and food to the furry among us while Jasper gets the two of us some hot apple cider.

We sit side by side on the sofa and Jasper pops open his briefcase, only to reveal a laptop with a bright orange sticker over it that reads *Sultan of Software*.

"Jasper, that's not your laptop," I say, leaning in to take a better look at the thing.

"No, it's not," he says. "It belonged to Barnabas Casper. Just picked it up this morning. I thought I'd go over it with a fine-tooth comb—under the guidance of the best detective I know."

"Oh, Jasper." I gasp as he pulls it forward and opens it up.

"I brought the charger in the event we need it, and judging by the sheer amount of files on this thing, we're going to need it. I did a quick once-over at the office."

"Crack it open," I say. "I can hardly wait."

Jasper is right. Barnabas has a plethora of files, and one by one, Jasper and I start to plow through them.

"Look at this one," Jasper points out after we've combed through two dozen files at least. Each file has the blueprint for the software design Barnabas was coding for them. "It's marked Drive. I bet we know which ex-boyfriend of yours that belongs to. Griffin the Octopus."

Sherlock barks as all three pets curl up by the crackling fire. *I tried to stop him, Jasper.*

Don't listen to him, Jasper, Fish mewls. *He's spinning a wagging dog* tale. She lashes Sherlock with her own tail. *You let the man hold you, for Pete's sake.*

Sherlock whines as he lays his head between his paws. *I couldn't help it. It was dark and scary.*

"It was dark and scary," I tell him. "Don't feel bad, Sherlock. Jasper knows you're loyal."

"That's right," Jasper says. "You're still my buddy. Griffin's not tearing this family apart, no matter what he might be thinking." He glances my way. "What exactly is he thinking?"

"It's probably best we don't go there."

"Okay." He sighs. "Let's finish straining these files through a mental sieve." He clicks into the Drive file and it's all pretty basic.

"Same cookie-cutter template for the most part that he's used on dozens of other files," I say just as something catches my eye. "What's STX?" The acronym runs down both pages of the software blueprint.

"I don't know. I don't remember seeing that in any other files."

"Huh." I snuggle up close to Jasper. "I bet Griffin would tell me if I asked."

"I bet Griffin would tell you or give you anything you ask." He wraps an arm around me and lands a kiss to the top of my head. "How about we take a break and talk about our suspects?"

"Sounds perfect. Let's start with Sabrina Chambers. Her father and Barnabas' father—the one who raised him—had it out in an ugly way."

"Her brother was killed in a freak accident—and it was her brother. She thought of him the day Barnabas died."

"Because they were the same age when they passed away. Far too young, by the way."

"What about Griffin?" Jasper growls when he says his name.

"He was friends with Barnabas, and is oddly protecting Sabrina from our spotlight, something fierce."

"You said he mentioned that Sabrina had been through enough?" he asks as he absentmindedly spins a soft circle in my hair.

"True, but he must sense she could be responsible. He kept trying to lead us to Carrie."

Jasper nods. "She's an easy target. She hated her half-brother."

I nod up at him. "And she had access to a marine biology lab via her sister." I take a sip of my cider. "How do you think Sabrina would have had access to the toxin that killed him?"

He blows out a breath. "I don't know. I'll have to haul her in for questioning. And after that, I'll haul in Carrie, too. It looks like my day is filling up tomorrow."

"Maybe wait a day on hauling them in until the day after. Tomorrow is Halloween. They're both scheduled to be at the Spider Cove Halloween Spooktacular. Griffin is holding a memorial of sorts for Barnabas, and I think Sabrina for sure will show up. I think Carrie will be there, too, but for entirely different reasons. The Red Riding Hood Society is meeting in the woods behind the gazebo. Besides, you don't want to miss the Howl-o-ween parade. Sherlock, Nutmeg, and Fish are all taking part in it. I'm even going to do my best to turn Sherlock into the biggest hunky chunk of bacon you ever did see."

"Sounds delicious." He lands a kiss on my nose. "I won't miss it."

"Good." I take another sip of my cider and glance at the animals as they snuggle near the flickering flames. "Nutmeg?"

She gives a lazy glance this way, her head heavy and her eyes even heavier.

"Did Barnabas ever say anything to you about Sabrina Chambers? She seems like such a wild card and I can't figure out why."

Sabrina? Her furry little ears perk up. *Oh, the one from the Montgomerys' farm. Every now and again Barnabas would drive out that way. They liked to rub noses, sort of the way the two of you do.*

That's their way of kissing, Fish says as she slices the air with her tail. *Humans think licking is for lollipops.*

I quickly translate for Jasper.

He waggles his brows my way before turning toward the fireplace. "Nutmeg? What about Justin Chambers? Sabrina's brother? Do you know anything about him?"

Justin? She sits up a notch. *They were friends. Sure, their families were on the outs, but they jogged together. I jogged with them, too. We should jog, Bizzy. You'll love it. Barnabas and I would run miles and miles. When he wasn't coding, he was running. That's why he got me. He wanted a running partner. He said I gave him a run for his money.* She gives a soft woof. *Barnabas didn't actually care for money. He said he saw what it did to people—how ugly they got when they got too much of it. He said he would be donating most of the money he got from the will. He wanted to give it to an animal shelter.*

I let Jasper know her thoughts.

He nods. "That would have been a great thing. I guess he really enjoyed what he did."

Nutmeg gives another soft bark. *He mostly did. He said he had a handful of greedy clients. Those he said he could live without, and that he was going to do just that.*

"Poor guy probably didn't get to do that either," I say as I pull out my phone. "Something about Sabrina and her brother is niggling at me." I look up Justin Chambers for myself and find a few scant pictures on social media.

Justin has a baby face, kind eyes, and full red lips. The picture of health. There's one picture in particular with him wearing a military jacket—dull green, across the right arm are two yellow stripes in a wide V, conjoined, like a couple of spooning arrow tips.

"Oh my"—I say, holding my phone where Jasper can see it —"that jacket. I've seen it before. I think this is the same jacket Barnabas was wearing the night he died."

159

Jasper examines it. "I think you're right. I wonder if Justin was in the Army?"

Nutmeg lifts her head. *He was in the service. I think he said he was a corporate.*

"Nutmeg says he was a corporate?"

Jasper nods. "A corporal. Of course, those stripes were telling the story."

"And now it makes sense why it looked as if Sabrina was trying to take off Barnabas' jacket just minutes before he was killed."

Jasper purses his lips. "Maybe it was just minutes before she killed him?"

"Maybe it was, but why? And how did she get the toxin?"

"Both questions we will answer." He puts the laptop down on the coffee table and runs his finger down the front of my dress. "But first, I think we have a wedding night to tend to."

"It's not yet evening," I muse.

"Then that gives us plenty of time to practice."

And practice we do.

CHAPTER 14

*H*alloween day has finally descended on Spider Cove as the crisp air crackles. The leaves have shriveled up and fallen from the maples that line Main Street and float through the air like orange confetti. A swell of excitement vibrates through our sleepy seaside community, and the underlying tension of evil pulsates here as well.

It's early evening, and the sun has just set, leaving the sky streaked with pink and deep purple hues. A jack-o'-lantern sits in front of every shop, and that giant pumpkin that stands taller than the gazebo at the end of the street glows with its own eerie grin.

Throngs of people have come out for the final string of parades that will eventually morph into an all-out party as the night wears on. Mayor Woods, my flirty sister-in-law, has set a strict timeline of events to keep the entire town entertained until one by one we surrender to the night.

First up is the parade of costumes for children under twelve, then comes the Howl-o-ween parade for all furry creatures big and small, and then the zombie walk will usher in the more frightening leg of the night—if those zombies don't eat that leg first and ruin things for the rest of us. Here's hoping the killer doesn't ruin things for the rest of us again, either. Although I'm more convinced than ever that whoever killed Barnabas Casper isn't interested in killing again. Or at least I hope not.

"Would you look at all these cute costumes?" I say to Macy who has somehow procured a small plastic pumpkin brimming with candy. "And hand me another one of those chocolate fun-size treats, would you?"

"Here." She hands me a Mr. Goodbar, and I gladly accept. "What cute costumes are you talking about? Everyone looks ridiculous."

Fish tries to swat the candy bar out of my hand, but I do my best to take a bite despite her disruptive efforts.

I'm sorry, Bizzy, but you specifically told me that if I saw you eating another piece of candy that I was to swat it out of your hands. That was a direct order, she mewls.

So it's true.

I wrinkle my nose at her. "I was kidding," I whisper.

"Of course, you're kidding." Macy snorts as we stand outside of our mother's shop and people-watch as the crowd seems to double in size every few minutes. "Check out all of these family costumes," she says the words *family costumes* in air quotes. "A family of wizards, a family of cowboys with red wigs and giant freckles? People with red hair and freckles should track down those cheap impersonators and sue. A family of superheroes, a family of baseball players, a family of astronauts, vampires, angels, skeletons, clowns, and hippies. And look over there at that family of wolves." She points across the way. "Speaking of which, I've got my robe in my tote bag for the big werewolf meet and greet later. I didn't want to compromise my look with a ratty old robe." She steps back and allows me to see the entirety of her work of genius.

Macy is wearing a black and white striped top hat, a black satin bustier with matching short-shorts, fishnets, and high heels, and not much else.

"What are you supposed to be again?"

Fish tips her head as she inspects her salty aunt. *I thought you said she was a honey trap.*

I did say that, and I think I'm right, but I'd like to know the official term per the honey trap's mouth.

"I'm the Mad Hatter." Macy lifts her hat before plunking it back over her head. "And what are you?" She frowns at the gown I'm currently drowning in.

Okay, so it's a bit big—like two dress sizes too big—but I bought it on triple clearance about six months ago. It's a red regency gown with light pink and white hearts printed all over it. The bodice is supposed to be fitted, and the skirt blossoms out with six different layers of ruffled fabric, giving it a glorious frilly appeal.

"I'm the Queen of Hearts. See?" I point to my cheeks where I've drawn a bright red heart over each one.

"Meh." Macy pretends to gag. "Have you ever wondered if you were adopted? I mean, you're nothing like Hux or me. You're a Miss Goody Two-Shoes through and through. Mom and Dad are both diabolical, and so none of us can figure out where you've come from."

"Macy." I laugh. "Our parents are not diabolical."

"Please." She scoffs. "While Mom was working her real estate empire, she was known as the Dragon. And Dad has been married close to a dozen times. You have to be diabolical in both of those situations. Hux is a shark by occupation. And I have a penchant for men. When have you ever been diabolical?"

I purse my lips. "Don't you think it's a coincidence that I'm the only one who ever finds a dead body around here?"

Fish sits up in my arms and snickers while Macy's face goes white.

"Is that a confession?" Macy wheezes just as Georgie, Juni, my mother, and three of the cutest little pooches you ever did see file out of the shop behind us.

"And that's a wrap," Mom chirps as she locks the door behind her. "We've sold more tombstones to the wives of this town than there are husbands!" Mom is dressed like the bride of Frankenstein, complete with a mummy-wrapped dress along with a black and white beehive wig that sits three feet off her head.

"Yup," Juni says while plucking a candy bar out of Macy's pumpkin. Juni has on a short dress with a tan animal print on it, fishnets, and sky-high red heels. "In fact, it was such a hit, a couple of customers begged us to have it as a year-round feature."

"Interesting," I say. "Juni, you look hot. What are you supposed to be?"

"I'm a cougar." She winks. "And you can bet your pink little hearts I'll be on the prowl for a younger man to snag for the night."

"That's my girl." Georgie pats her on the back. "Stalking your prey just the way I taught ya." Georgie is wearing a black and orange kaftan and has her eyelids encrusted with glittery pink eye shadow. "And before you ask, I'm a wise old woman. After wearing a costume for the last thirty days straight, I've decided to be the scariest creature of them all—myself."

Mom bucks with a laugh. "Apparently, you're a wise old woman who tells the truth."

"Never mind all that," Macy says, handing each one of them a piece of candy. "I just got a confession out of my little diabolical sister. Bizzy has just confessed to being the Spider Cove Strangler."

Sherlock gives a few aggressive barks up at me. *Take it back, Bizzy. I thought we agreed if you ever confessed you'd only tell your secret to me.*

And me, Fish growls. *You said only we would know where the bodies were buried.*

"I was kidding," I say to those human and not.

Sherlock, Nutmeg, Candy, and Fish are all in costume themselves. Believe it or not, I was able to procure a bacon costume yesterday online, and it showed up just as we were about to leave the cottage this morning. So Sherlock is living the dream.

Nutmeg decided she wanted to pair up with him, so she's donned a couple of sunny-side up eggs over her back—large fabric eggs that both Sherlock and Candy have both tried to eat several times today.

Macy has dressed Candy in a hot pink tutu and white feathered angel wings—something she confessed to pulling straight from her nightclub stash.

And, of course, Fish hasn't been left out of the fun. She's donned a pair of bunny ears and called it a day. After a month of tormenting her with every costume imaginable, I agreed to this one mercy she asked for. All four of the pets are focused one hundred percent on the parade of littles that are marching up the street, each one looking as cute as a Halloween button. I can't blame anyone for gawking at them. It's hard to look away from such adorableness.

Macy groans, "And would you look at that zombie heading this way holding that screaming baby? You'd think some parents would have better judgment than to get that gory while minding an infant."

Mom's mouth falls open. "That's no zombie. That's your brother."

Huxley enters our midst in a flannel and jeans, not his usual attire of a sharp suit that we're used to seeing him in. He has dark bags under his eyes, a full-blown beard on his face, and his hair is slightly mussed.

"Oh, come here, honey." Mom takes the baby from his arms and quickly soothes my sweet nephew. Baby Mack is dressed as a polar bear in a white fuzzy suit with a hood with an adorable face on it. The poor baby hiccups away while clinging to my mother as if she was his new favorite blanket. Hux hands my mother a bottle, much to the baby's delight and all is right with the world again.

"Huxley." I give him a quick hug. "How are things going?" I wince as I ask. Obviously, he looks wrecked so I can only surmise.

"I don't sleep." He moans. "I don't shower. I'm not sure when the last time I ate was."

"Eat now," Macy says, shoving a handful of candy his way and Hux quickly unwraps five miniature candy bars and shoves them into his mouth.

"Macy, where did you get that pumpkin, anyway?" I ask. "Is it from your store? Is that the free candy you were giving to your customers?"

Just about every shop in Spider Cove has had a pumpkin full of candy for their patrons this month so it wouldn't surprise me.

"Why would I give free candy to my customers?" she balks. "Do I look like I run a charity to you?"

"There it is, Mommy!" A little boy dressed as a purple alien with one giant eyeball painted onto his forehead rushes his mother this way. "That's my pumpkin, and that mean old woman stole it!"

The mother gives a tight smile as she removes the pumpkin from Macy's hands and briskly walks her child into the crowd.

"Who are you calling old, kid?" Macy shouts after them.

"Macy!" I bump her arm with mine. "Did you steal that kid's Halloween candy?"

"Of course not. I found it sitting on the table outside my shop. I believe that fell under the finders keepers, losers weepers law."

Hux nods with a mouthful. "That would be correct."

"And cruel," I note just as the crowd collectively coos at a congregation of preschoolers slogging along the parade route.

"I'd better get going," Macy says, craning her neck. "I need to find my mark for the night before all the good ones are taken. Make sure to get lots of pictures of Candy during the parade, would you? I'll see you both in the woods for the encounter of the howling kind." She blows Candy a kiss before disappearing into the crowd.

"Wait for me, kid!" Juni trots after her as fast as her heels will allow. *Macy always gets the good ones. But not tonight. I'm determined to go younger and hotter than ever before. And the best way to do that is to follow the dust Macy kicks up from her man-eating heels.*

I shrug over at my brother. "So where's your other half?" I'd say *better half*, but I wouldn't mean it. The fact Mackenzie has been a hands-off mother doesn't exactly sit well with me.

"I don't know. Wherever your ex-boyfriend is, I'm assuming. Mackenzie had dinner with him last night and breakfast with him this morning." *If she didn't come home last night, I would have drawn up the divorce papers and served them to her before lunch. For the life of me, I can't figure out why she's so willing to throw us away. Maybe Mom is right. Maybe she's having some sort of a postpartum breakdown, and it's just harder to identify because this is Mackenzie we're talking about. I need to give her space. Mom says she'll come around and dote on the baby in no time. Heck, at this point I'd be happy if she'd acknowledge the baby. How can she not love that face? I've never been more in love with a human in all my life. In fact, I'd give my life for his. And apparently, I'm doing just that. I don't mind. But I sure could use a little help.*

"Oh, Hux." My heart hurts just hearing his thoughts. "How about this? Tonight is the last of the chaos that's overrun the inn. I have nothing planned in the weeks ahead, would you mind if I babysat my sweet nephew for a few days a week? I could even come over for an hour or two each day so you could, you know, shave, shower, and eat a decent meal?"

"I'm in, too," Mom says as she strides up while rocking the baby. "I told you from the beginning I would do that, Hux."

"I know." He squeezes his eyes shut tight. "And I'm ready to take you both up on it. Maybe you can work something out where you're each over every other day. That way I still have someone to lean on each day and you're not getting burnt out."

"I would never get burnt out," I tell him. "If anything, baby Mack is going to make me want a baby of my own more than ever before."

He gives a mournful chuckle. "Babies are a lot of work, Biz." He glances to Mack as he falls asleep over my mother's shoulder. "But they are worth every minute of it."

A man dressed as Frankenstein's monster heads this way, staggering with his arms outstretched, but once he spots me, his green face goes sallow.

Good grief, there she is, the little Grim Reaper dressed in hearts—the hearts of her victims no less.

My mother's boyfriend marches over and lands a kiss to her cheek.

"Hello, everyone." He gives a curt nod my way and hiccups. *I'd best be kind to her lest my own heart ends up on her sleeve. And the longer I spend time in this creepy town, the more assured I am of that misfortune.*

Geez, Brennan is terrified of me.

"Hello, Brennan." I give a friendly wave. "I'm so glad to see you. I've missed you these past few weeks. Where have you been hiding out?" I tease.

Fish chortles. *The man looks ready to run, Bizzy.*

Georgie steps forward. "Yeah, Gallagher, where have you been hiding?" She gives him the stink eye. "So help me the Great Pumpkin, if I find out you've been messing around behind Preppy's back, right under her nose. You'd better high-tail it out of town if you even look at Preppy crooked. She's got a killer daughter in her back pocket and a bestie who knows how to hide a body."

"Aww," Mom coos as she looks to Georgie. "You'd help me hide his body?"

"Darn tootin'," Georgie says before looking my way. "Try to keep it neat. I don't look forward to getting blood under my nails."

Hux nods. "I'm with Georgie. Stay away from leaving any DNA at the scene of the crime. If things go south, I'll have an easier time defending you."

"Holy hiccups." Brennan's body bucks with a hiccup as he says it. *They're plotting my demise right here in the open. No wonder I've had these annoying body malfunctions happening for the last two weeks solid.* He jerks with another hiccup. *My poor mother always did say it was a sign that someone is thinking ill will for you. I can't deny it any longer. My life will come to an unfortunate demise if I stick around this haunted town another minute. I'd best pack it up and head back to Scotland. I wonder if Rose Alice ever married? She was a good God-fearing girl, and she had the hots for me something awful before I left for the states. As much as I like Ree, I like breathing a little bit more. I'd give my life for the woman, but not as a sacrifice to her bloodthirsty children.*

"I think I left the stove on," Brennan says as he staggers backward. "I'll be back soon enough." He gives my mother a look that suggests otherwise.

"What?" Mom balks as she hands the baby back to my brother. "But I was the last to leave the house. And I always make sure the stove is off," she says, traipsing after him, but

Brennan is staggering quickly through the crowd, and an entire gaggle of children scream at the sight of him.

"Would you get back here?" Mom calls out. "I'm going to lose you if you don't slow down."

"Oh no," I moan. "I think maybe Mom has already lost Brennan."

"*Eh.*" Georgie shrugs. "Easy come, easy go. The guy was lousy in bed."

"*Ew,*" I say as both Hux and I cringe. "Keep the details to yourself."

"Yes." Hux winces. "Whatever our mother told you was for your ears only."

"She didn't tell me anything," Georgie says. "I've been doing a little amateur sleuthing myself. I've got an upside-down apple crate outside their bedroom window and I'm not afraid to use it. Now that the show is over, I can finally get a decent night's sleep." She sniffs the air. Well, well... I smell a hairy, scary beast. It seems the werewolves will be coming out to play after all. I'll see you in the woods, Toots. Don't be late if you want a furry date." She takes off.

"I won't be going," I tell Fish. "I've already got a furry date, times four."

"Me, too." Hux gives me a quick embrace. "We're out of here. I'll see you soon, sis."

"Love you both," I shout as they take off.

Sherlock barks. *I smell a beast, too. It's that lowlife, Griffin, and he's right across the street.*

Nutmeg cranes her furry little head. *And he's with that sister-in-law of yours.*

I glance across the street, and sure enough, there they are, standing right outside of Lather and Light, schmoozing and canoodling with their heads knit close as if they were a couple.

"Great," I mutter. "Mackenzie is doing her level best to torpedo her marriage, and Griffin isn't exactly helping. Although, if I go over, he'll probably think I want him all to myself. But I am happily taken. Speaking of my man, tell me if any of you see Jasper. He's dressed as a dashing homicide detective," I say as I stand on my tiptoes and observe the crowd. "He said the full lab analysis of the toxin came in, and he was hoping it might pinpoint where the killer got the compound."

"Killer?" a light voice chirps from behind, and I spot Carrie Hazelman looking stunning with her red velvet cloak pulled over her head as if she was ready and willing to summon a werewolf right this minute. "Are you talking about Barnabas' killer?" She blinks at me as she asks. "I'm sorry, I wasn't trying to listen in on your phone conversation. I was just walking by when I happened to hear it."

I wasn't on the phone. I was talking to my animals, but I'll go along with her theory for now.

"No, actually, they haven't caught the killer. But I hear they're trying to trace the compound that was used to kill him in hopes to find out where the killer procured the toxin."

She tips her head back. "You know, I've thought about it, and I know how the killer got their hands on that toxin."

Fish sits straight up and bops me in the face with her bunny ears.

She's going to confess, Fish yowls. *Quick, turn on your phone and record it. I want to be done with this. I want to be done with this entire day. Is it Christmas yet?*

My cheek tugs to the side. She's not alone with the sentiment.

"How?" I ask the blonde before me. "How did the killer get their hands on that toxin?"

"She works for the Montgomerys, and I happen to know they have a sustainable sea farm right here off the coast. They grow all sorts of sea vegetables, but mostly organic seaweed. It's a big deal. I've been thinking about heading over and doing a few shoots for my Insta Pictures account. My followers love that sort of thing. Anyway, she's your killer."

But why would she kill him? Fish balks.

"Yes, why would Sabrina kill Barnabas? I mean, they were dating. It couldn't have ended that badly."

Carrie tips her head. "But it did. It ended in death. Her brother, Justin, was killed at a party a while back. Some Roman rocket firework blasted a hole right through his chest."

"But it was an accident?" It comes out more of a question.

She shrugs. "Maybe. According to the rumor mill, she and Barn just broke up because he cheated on her. Justin went over and threatened to ruin Barnabas for ruining his sister and a fight ensued. The fight was broken up, but later that night, guess who was holding that Roman rocket when it went off?"

"Barnabas?" I ask, blown away by the thought.

She gives a quick nod. "And guess who handed me the cupcake to shove in his face that night?"

Sabrina?

I take in a quick breath, and Carrie's lips curl as she gives the revelation.

"I'll see you in the woods in a bit," she says, cinching her robe around her tight. "Try not to bring the dogs this time. As much as I love the four-footed among us, I love howling at the moon on Halloween night just a little bit more. And with any luck, I won't be howling alone." She takes off before I can stop her.

"We need to talk to Sabrina."

I call Sherlock, Nutmeg, and Candy over and enlist their people-sniffing superpowers until we come upon the exact woman I want to speak with as she stands near the gazebo just shy of the giant pumpkin threatening to eat the town.

The redhead turns my way abruptly and smiles. "Oh, my word! Look at all this cuteness you've got with you!" She gives each dog a quick pat then a heartier rub to Fish's back.

Sabrina is dressed as a police officer in a blue skimpy uniform that happens to be low-cut and comes with a tiny skirt to boot. A pair of silver cuffs swings from her hip, and I can tell by the way they sway in the breeze they're plastic and not at all like the real deal she might be all too familiar with by the end of the night.

Call Jasper! Sherlock barks, and I pull out my phone but hesitate.

"Sabrina," her name expels from me in a mournful sigh. Griffin was right. This poor girl has been through so much already. "Why did you do it?"

Her mouth rounds out. "Oh, this?" She pinches at her skirt. "I know. My mother tried to stop me as I was leaving the house. She said I looked like a prostitute hoping to service the station, rather than a crime hunter." She laughs. "Oh, well. I'll plan better for next year." She cranes her neck past me. "Can you believe how delicious those cupcakes are? And to think they're free." She shakes her head. *I'm going to eat ten if I don't eat an even dozen.*

I glance to where Emmie is working with a few members of our staff, handing out the sweet treats to the public. Leo is there with them, and he's keeping an extra eye out in the event the killer decides to strike again.

"They are delicious," I say. "Sabrina, I wasn't talking about your costume. Why did you exact revenge on Barnabas? Surely there were other ways to help deal with your loss." My voice comes out pleading, but it's too late for her to turn back any of her actions now.

The redhead blinks over at me, stunned. "Excuse me?"

"The day of the murder, Barnabas caught your eye—but only because he was wearing that military jacket. It belonged to your brother, didn't it?"

"Yes." Her eyes squeeze shut. "It was Justin's jacket. Justin gave it to Barnabas. They were good friends—or so Justin thought."

I nod. "I heard that Barnabas cheated on you."

Her eyes widen. "He did cheat on me. It was horrible." She shudders just as a scream comes from somewhere in the crowd. "I hope you never live through that kind of pain, Bizzy. A part of me wondered if it was Barn who was exacting revenge—on my family via my heart." She closes her eyes, the pain on her face palpable. "I hated him."

"And your brother hated him, too, after that, didn't he?" My voice is soft and tender. I don't want to bring this woman any more grief.

She swallows hard. "It's true. Justin said he was going to kill him." Her chest bounces with a dry laugh. "But Barnabas beat him to it. I'm not sure if you know this, but my brother died because a firework malfunctioned." She says that last word in air quotes. "Barnabas was holding the device. He had a friend light it. He was supposed to point it to the sky and he pointed it at my brother instead. He killed my brother that night. And I'd like to think Barnabas' death, as tragic as it was —well, there was a little cosmic justice involved."

"By way of your own hand?" I tip my head, anticipating what she might say—or think.

She blinks back. "Why would you say that?"

"Carrie said you handed her the cupcake that she smashed into his face. That cupcake was laced with a toxin found in sea life. Sabrina, I just found out your employer, the Montgomerys, has a sea farm."

"I don't know what you're trying to imply, lady, but I didn't kill Barnabas that night. Besides, I didn't even handle the cupcake for long. Someone handed it to me."

"Who?" I ask, hoping to catch her off guard and dislodge a thought that could cinch her guilt.

"I don't know, whoever was standing next to me. I can't remember. If you'll excuse me, I need two dozen cupcakes to dissolve this conversation from my mind." *If I killed Barnabas, it would have been with a flaming arrow through his heart, not some sweet confection that he probably enjoyed on its way down.*

She takes off, and I'm left standing there trying to digest this.

"She didn't do it." I blow out a sigh.

A tall man with hairy scruff on his cheeks and a devil may care smile is about to stride by when I intercept him.

"Gentry!" I run up, and he laughs as he playfully wrestles with the dogs. "Gentry, you were with Barnabas in those last few moments. Do you remember who was standing at the dessert table with him before he ate that ill-fated cupcake?"

He glances to the sky. "I don't, sorry, Bizzy. There were a lot of people here that day. He was with that redhead you were just talking with, and Carrie was there." His head tips side to side. "A tall man with dark hair and a suit was there, too."

"Well, thank you anyway." My shoulders sag at the thought of hitting another dead end.

Bizzy? Fish taps my chest with her paw. ***Didn't the deceased do some work for this man? Maybe he can tell you what that mysterious acronym means, the one that was vexing you all night.***

I nod. "Gentry, I got ahold of some personal files that belonged to Barnabas, and I have a question I'm hoping you can answer."

"Anything," he says, picking up Nutmeg and landing a kiss to her forehead. "Shoot." He mock shoots me with his fingers. "Except with silver bullets, of course." He gives a sly wink.

"Funny," I say. "Jasper and I found the letters *STX* in some of his clients' files, and we couldn't for the life of us figure out what they meant."

"Ah." He rocks back on his heels, and the look of discontent crosses his face. "I know exactly what it stands for because he tried to sell me on it. I guess he had a prominent client who swore by it. STX stands for surtax. Barnabas was coding bogus taxes into the system and lining someone's pocket with some dishonest green. Anyway"—he gives Nutmeg a friendly pat as he puts her down—"I'm off to call my men. The girls have been faithful." He shrugs. "I think we'll make an appearance tonight." He strides off, and I'm left in a dust storm of thoughts.

Sabrina said someone handed her that cupcake… Gentry said he saw a tall man in a suit there… And STX is essentially stolen money.

It all comes to me at once as the final pieces of the puzzle snap into place.

My phone buzzes in my pocket, and I pull it out.

It's a text from Jasper.

Just pulled into the driveway. I'll walk down and meet up with you. I know where the toxin came from, and I have a feeling I know who the killer is.

I nod as I look out at the crowd.

I have a feeling I know who the killer is, too.

My feet move me in the direction of Lather and Light.

And I've got a few burning questions to ask him.

CHAPTER 15

*T*he sky darkens to soot as the orange and white twinkle lights dance from one streetlamp to the other, casting their soft glow over the thicket of people who have come out to celebrate this fiendishly nefarious night.

One thing is for sure, Halloween in Spider Cove is shaping up to be a scary one.

I'm about to cross the street when Candy blocks my path with that enormous hot pink tutu of hers.

You don't need to take another step. Candy barks my way.

She's right! Sherlock gives a terse growl from behind me, and Nutmeg joins him in the effort.

Fish peers over my shoulder, and her bunny ears flop to the side. *Oh, brother.* She moans. *Here we go.*

I turn around just in time to see Griffin Duncan standing there holding a cupcake in each hand. He's dressed in a strange uniform, and he has a sash across his chest that reads *Prince Charming.*

"Wow, it's almost as if you read my mind and knew I was about to call out for you," he muses. *If she could read my mind, she'd be thrilled to know I was looking forward to making her every dream come true.*

I take in a quick breath. He's out of his mind. And for once, I'm going to judge a person for their thoughts. Griffin is a delusional idiot if he thinks for a minute that I'd leave Jasper for him. I didn't chase after him when he left me for Mackenzie, and I certainly am not chasing after him now. *Especially* now.

He thrusts a cupcake my way. "For you, my queen."

"Thank you." I take it from him with zero intention of taking a single bite. Not after the knowledge I just procured. "Griffin, we need to talk. It's very important."

"Important?" He drinks me in. "You look as if you've got big news."

"In a way, I do."

His eyes widen as he takes me in anew. "In that case, let's go someplace where we can be alone. The music, the screaming kids, it's all eating up my eardrums and I can hardly hear you."

He grabs ahold of my waist and hastily navigates us past

the giant pumpkin and right to the mouth of the woods where it's cooler and just a touch quieter.

"Jasper will be here any minute," I say, panting as I take him in.

He groans, "Well, then we'd better make a run for it while there's still time," he teases.

Sherlock gives a few aggressive barks, and both Nutmeg and Candy take a defensive stance on either side of him.

Griffin lifts a hand to pet Fish, but she swats him away with a soft hiss.

His eyes narrow over her. *That cat will be the first to go when Bizzy and I start our new life together.*

"Before you say anything"—he runs his hand over my hair, and I freeze solid from his touch—"I just put a down payment on a house not too far from the inn. Well, if you can call an eight thousand square foot structure a mere house. It's bordering on a mansion. I wanted to ask if you'd help me decorate. The inn looks so homey and great, I think this place could really use your touch, Bizzy." *And I can use your touch, too.* His brows do a little dance with the suggestive thought. *By the time I'm through wooing her, she'll be begging me to off the detective. Not that he'll last that long. She'll need to be a widow for a few weeks at least before I swoop in for the kill.*

Off the detective? I inch back. A widow?

My goodness, this man is out to kill my husband.

"What's the matter?" He leans in, his eyes heavy with concern. "You look like you've just seen a ghost."

"More like a monster," I say.

My blood boils at the thought of Griffin plotting to kill the man I'd give my own life for.

"Pardon?" He tips his ear my way.

"I had heard that Barnabas had a handful of greedy clients," I say, unable to take my eyes away from the boy I once knew.

Nutmeg prances around in a circle. *That was me! I said that.*

I nod to Griffin. "But I wouldn't have guessed in a million years that you would have been one of them."

Griffin juts his chin forward. "What's that?"

"You had told me that Barnabas was your good friend, that he knew all of your secrets…" A laugh lives and dies in my chest. "And now I know exactly what secrets you were talking about."

He glances past me as if struggling to keep up. "I'm sorry, Bizzy. I'm afraid I don't understand."

"By all means, let me help with that." I take a deep breath. "The day Barnabas died, you were so quick to point the finger at Sabrina. Even before we knew there was a homicide to investigate. But your guilt was eating away at you because you actually felt sorry for Sabrina, so you changed your tune. You hinted Gentry might have done it. In fact, you hinted that the very night of the murder as well. And then, in time, you threw Carrie under the bus. All of that finger-pointing should have tipped me off."

His lips flicker. "Tipped you off to what?" *There's no way in hell Bizzy has figured it out. She's not that smart.*

"You wish," I mutter. "The night we had dinner at Lucky Thirteen, you mentioned that Barnabas worked on the software for your company, Drive. I should have paid closer attention to that. You were delivering the mother of all clues on a silver platter—and you handed it right to us."

His left eye comes shy of winking. "What clue?"

"The day we were having lunch out on Main Street, you

mentioned that Barnabas Casper made you a very rich man." I nod. "And as it turns out, he did indeed."

"Oh, that." A relieved bout of laughter erupts from him. "It's true as gospel." Griffin holds up his hands. *If only she knew how true it was.* "So what's the big news? Did you figure out who the killer is?" *She couldn't have.*

"But I could have. That's exactly what my big news is."

His lips curve at the thought. "All right, I give. Who do you think did it?"

Oh, he's condescending, isn't he? Fish growls. *Tell him what you know and leave the rest to me.*

"You did it," I say it loud and proud—and more than ready to take Fish up on her offer.

"Me?" Griffin rocks back on his heels. "This is rich. Let's hear what you've got." *There is no way she has any evidence to pin this on me. I've covered my tracks. I'm practically a pro. They won't catch me. And when I kill her husband—they won't catch me then either.*

"You are not touching a hair on Jasper Wilder's head." My voice shakes as I step his way, and he slowly backs into the woods. "You killed Barnabas Casper because he was about to turn you over to the authorities, wasn't he? He knew that the surtax that you probably had him embed into your systems was perfectly illegal. It could have landed you both in prison —but now it's only going to take you there."

Griffin grows rigid. Long shadows take over his features, and any trace of the handsome man he is dissipates. Griffin looks marred, ugly, and deformed as he glares right at me.

"And you handed Sabrina that poisoned cupcake to give to him. I wondered how you did it, how anyone could have gotten their hands on that toxin. You tried to hand-feed me the fact it was Carrie—but it was you. Lucky Thirteen has an extensive seafood menu, and your own *wife* said you had a hand in picking up the freshest foods for the establishment right down to the seaweed. That's how you did it. And that's why you did it. You're a killer, Griffin. You need to confess."

All traces of a smile dissolve from his face. "Wow, you are good. Yes, I had Barn add a surtax to my software. What's wrong with that?"

"When you don't report it to the customer *or* the IRS, it's a very big problem."

"So what? I can handle the IRS. I just needed a little time. Barnabas wanted to extort money from me. He wasn't a good guy, Bizzy. If you only knew the things he did, you wouldn't care that I fed him a bucket full of poison." He squeezes his eyes shut tight.

"I don't care about his sins. You should have let the law take care of that."

"I needed to take care of it before things got out of hand," he riots back, and the dogs go wild.

Easy, buddy, Fish hisses right at him. *Nobody talks to my girl that way.*

"Oh, shut up," he grouses at Fish. "Look, Bizzy. Why don't we head back to my place? I'll tell you everything right from the beginning." *I can slip something into her drink and have us to Canada before she wakes up. I'm not losing Bizzy again. If I'm going on the lam, I'm taking her with me.*

"I'm not going anywhere with you."

"Darn right you're not," a deep voice strums from behind, and I turn to see my true Prince Charming looking dashing in a dark suit with a pale yellow tie that brings out those lightning bolts in his eyes.

"He confessed," I say to Jasper. "He killed Barnabas."

"You'll never prove it." Griffin laughs. "I never handed Barn that cupcake."

"You're right," I tell him. "You handed it to Sabrina, and she handed it to Carrie. Gentry James saw the whole thing play about. And he knows all about your fake surtax as well. The jury will find him a credible witness." Maybe that last bit is true, but I may have embellished the rest.

"Geez." Griffin rakes his fingers through his hair. "Why did you have to dig, Bizzy?" he riots at me, and I'm seeing a far meaner, far more volatile version of the boy I once knew. "We could have had everything," he pants wildly. "I'm not letting you ruin this." He grabs ahold of my wrist. "You're coming with me."

"Over my dead body," Jasper snaps as he yanks me back.

"As you wish, buddy," Griffin says as he throws a wild punch, hitting Jasper right in the temple and sending him staggering.

A shrill scream escapes me as Jasper struggles to remain on his feet.

All three dogs go on the attack as Jasper steps forward and takes a quick breath.

"Down, all of you," he says while glaring at Griffin. "I've got this one."

In less than a second, Jasper and Griffin are exchanging powerful blows, and I'm screaming my head off as if my hair was on fire.

Leo runs this way at top speed and stops abruptly as he witnesses the carnage playing out.

"Do something," I shout, but Leo simply shrugs as we watch Jasper pummel the heck out of Griffin's face.

"Let's let him get his aggression out a bit." Leo chuckles. "Jasper told me all about the slime."

After thirty seconds more of the beatdown, Leo steps in, and soon he has Griffin in handcuffs.

"I'm sorry, Bizzy," Griffin says through a cut and bloodied lip. "We would have been good together."

"No, we wouldn't have," I tell him. "We were never meant to be. If we were, you would never have cheated all those years ago to begin with."

Leo carts him off before he can respond, and I pull Jasper to me.

Fish yowls, *Go ahead and kiss the man. He did what I could only hope to do. Although, I could have done extensive damage with my claws.*

I would have torn him to pieces if Jasper hadn't shown. Sherlock barks, and both Nutmeg and Candy share his sentiment.

"You're a real hero," I say as I land a lingering kiss to my handsome hubby's lips.

He shakes his head. "You're the hero, and we both know it. If I'm not careful, you're going to steal my job."

"I don't want your job. I just want you."

We share another kiss under the full Halloween moon as a series of wild howls light up the night.

Lucky for me, I'll have Jasper Wilder forever.

CHAPTER 16

"Great news, Bizzy!" Georgie shouts as she heads our way.

The Howl-o-ween parade is getting ready to begin, and Jasper and I are standing near the back of the processional with him holding Sherlock's leash and me holding onto Nutmeg and Candy. Fish is in my arms. She'd rather be carried than jog with the dogs—her words, not mine.

"What's going on?" I ask as Georgie runs up winded.

"I've decided to join the zombie walk again." She hitches her head toward the woods. "You know what they say—if you fall off a dead body, just climb back on and keep riding. I may have lost my partner, but I haven't lost my mind, and that's something to celebrate."

"Good for you, Georgie," Jasper says. "In fact, if you need a partner, I'll team up with you."

"Me, too," I offer.

"Thanks, but I've already got a partner. He's tall, dark, and he's not just merely dead, he's deader than a doornail, if you know what I mean. He says he just crawled out of the cemetery this afternoon."

"Lovely," I muse.

It's Halloween night, and the crowd here on Main Street only seems to grow denser by the minute.

A familiar witch strides our way, and suddenly there aren't enough people to block her from our view.

"Camila," I say as she comes upon us. "You look perfectly green with envy this evening."

She waves me off. "I was just about to head to the inn when I spotted all those patrol cars leaving. I take it Jasper found the killer?" She lifts a brow as if trying to get him to admit to the fact it was me who found them.

For someone who is continuously accusing me of emasculating my husband, she sure does a pretty good job on her own.

"We both found the killer," I say. "Jasper beat him to a pulp."

"Because I had to," Jasper adds. *And wanted to.*

Mackenzie stomps over with a look of marked agitation in her beady eyes.

"Bizzy Baker," she barks. "What's this I hear about Griffin's arrest? Are you trying to sabotage my relationship with him?"

"Relationship?" I balk. "Mackenzie, you're married to my brother. And you have a child together, in the event you've forgotten."

She turns her cheek as if I struck her. "Of course, I haven't forgotten. I just meant that Griffin and I were kicking off our friendship once again. It's nice to have someone to talk to who isn't constantly badgering me to change a dirty diaper. I miss adult conversation, and Griffin was good at it."

Jasper nods. "He was good at murder, too. He's headed to the station right now, and they're going to book him."

"Murder?" She clasps her throat with her hand. *My goodness, I almost left Hux for a murderer. That lunatic could have hurt my child. I could have brought disaster on my entire family.* Her lips stiffen as she looks my way. "Never mind that. Christmas is coming and so is my cousin Felicity."

"Felicity?" I chime. "I love your cousin Felicity." She's our age as well, but she went to a private school two towns over, so we didn't see each other that often. Felicity is so sweet and kind, it's a miracle she and Mackenzie are related at all.

"I love her, too." Mack nods. "Her fiancé just proposed a few nights ago, and she's throwing together an impromptu wedding at the beginning of December. She said she wanted to get married in a haunted house, so I immediately volunteered your haunted inn. I told her she could host it there, all expenses paid."

"Haunted house?" I take a moment to frown at her. "You're lucky I'm open that month," I tell her. "And you're lucky I like Felicity enough to comp all costs. Oh, a holiday wedding," I beam as I look up at Jasper. "I cannot wait for the fun to begin."

"I'll need the Country Cottage Café to cater, of course," Mackenzie barrels on. "And Cider Cove will be hosting *A Night in Bethlehem* the night before Christmas Eve as well. All of Main Street will be transformed into that manger-riddled town. The chamber of commerce is sponsoring the event, and we're looking into procuring dozens of camels, donkeys, and an entire slew of mangy menageries that belong in a manger."

"Mackenzie," I balk. "You can't fit dozens of large animals on Main Street—not to mention the crowds they'll bring in. I don't think it'll be safe."

"You're right." She points my way. "We'll need use of the clearing in front of the inn."

"*No* to the clearing," I tell her.

She waves me off. "We'll talk. Every business owner and resident in Cider Cove is invited to the event and we expect quite a turnout. I'm sure I'll see all of you there. I'd better get home." She glances around at the crowd. "I need to hold baby Mack extra tight. I feel like we've escaped a madman."

"And you have," I say.

Mackenzie zips away, and I lean into Jasper.

"Hopefully, she'll appreciate her family just a little bit more." I sigh. "I can't believe how much destruction Griffin almost caused."

Georgie groans, "Speaking of destruction, here comes Hurricane Ree."

Mom stomps over with her black and white wig following her like a dark cloud hovering above her head.

"We need another tombstone," she growls.

"For who?" I ask, pulling her close.

"*Pfft.*" Georgie yanks my mother over to her. "And they say you're a mind reader. She needs the tombstone for that louse that left her for an airline stewardess in a little short skirt."

"Brennan left you?" Jasper looks at my mother, shocked by this turn of events. I probably should have clued him in on the warning signs.

"Wait!" Macy calls out as she clip-clops her way over. "Did I hear you right?" She looks to our mother. "Did Brennan turn into the flying Scotsman?"

Mom makes a face. "You heard right." She shakes her head at Georgie. "But he didn't leave me for some stewardess."

Georgie waves her off. "Only because he hasn't met her yet. Give him two hours, an international airport, a plane ticket in his pocket, and a glass full of whiskey in his belly. They'll be hot and heavy before the wheels touch down on the Emerald Isle—or is it the Tartan Isle? Anyway, he's moved on and so should you. But don't you worry, Preppy. It's your lucky night. It's a full moon, we've got our red robes handy"— she pats the tote bag by her side—"and an entire bushel of hairy beasts are about to come out to party with us. You're going to have a wild and wooly time. You'll show that louse what you're made of—revenge sex."

"Would you stop," Mom wails. "I'm not sleeping with a werewolf just to make myself feel better after my boyfriend up and left the country." She makes a face. *Although if the night goes on, I might just let her talk me into it.*

I make a face.

The Howl-o-ween parade commences, and we walk as a group along with our furry friends.

Sherlock and Nutmeg proudly display their bacon and egg duo. Candy and Macy look… well, they look like a couple of call girls.

Fish stands proud in my arms, turning her head to the right and left so everyone on both sides of the street can get a gander at her adorable little bunny ears.

And before we know it, we come to the end of Main Street, right where it meets up with that giant pumpkin with its friendly smile, as a raucous applause breaks out for all the adorable pets at hand.

"And that's a wrap," I say just as Emmie and Leo head our way.

Emmie is dressed as a vampire queen with her collar up over her ears, her face paper-white, and a trail of blood dripping down her chin. She's got both her dog and Leo's on leashes, a labradoodle named Cinnamon and a golden retriever named Gatsby, and they both have black capes on as well.

"We missed it!" Emmie cries as she stomps her foot. "Darn it. I thought I'd have time to run back and get them."

Not to worry, Sherlock says as he breaks free from Jasper's grasp and encourages the rest of the furry among us to do the same. *We'll take a quick victory lap. Come on.*

The dogs take off, and we watch as they race down the middle of the parade route once again.

Leo pats Jasper on the shoulder. "You really nailed that guy in the face. He looked like a raw steak when you were through with him. Remind me not to tick you off."

Emmie laughs, then stops abruptly. "If you so much as touch my husband's face, I'll be forced to return the favor." She gives the mild threat with a smile as she looks to Jasper. "But that won't happen because Leo isn't a killer." She wraps her arms around me. "And I hear someone here has caught the latest killer to stalk our streets." She pecks a kiss to my cheek. "I'm so glad you're safe. Griffin Duncan always did give me the creeps. He didn't hurt you, did he?"

I shake my head, but before I can extrapolate, the dogs run

back in a barking, jumping, happy pack, and along with them a furry man with a mischievous gleam in his eyes.

"Hey, Gentry," I say as he comes this way.

"Good show," he says with a laugh. "So what's to become of this cute little one?" He taps Nutmeg over the side. "Barn really did love her."

"I don't know," I tell him. "No one has come forth to claim her."

He gives a wistful tick of his furry head. "What if I claimed her? I think it's about high time my kind makes peace with these beautiful creatures. And I'd love to have her."

Really? Nutmeg barks and yips with glee. *Can I, Bizzy? Can I go with Gentry and have a home of my own again?*

"It's fine by me," I say. "That's just another reason I get to visit Glimmerspell."

Me, too! Sherlock barks.

Me three, Candy chirps.

Me four, Fish mewls. *Good luck in your new home, Nutmeg. I'm sorry to see you go.*

All five of the dogs begin to howl at once, and the sound echoes into the night.

The sound of chanting erupts from somewhere deep in the woods as the words *I'm not afraid of the Big Bad Wolf* are heard over and over again, faster and faster.

"Oh, they're starting," Mom says as she grabs ahold of Georgie and they take off.

"Wait for me," Macy calls out as she looks my way. "Mind Candy for me, would you?"

"Yes, of course. Go, go," I tell her as she takes off. "And I'll watch Nutmeg for you, too. For the entire night," I say to Gentry. "Have a good time out there. And Happy *Howl*-o-ween."

He barks out a laugh. "Happy Howl-o-ween right back at you. I'll see you at the inn in the morning."

He takes off in one direction, and Jasper, Emmie, Leo, and our menagerie head in the direction of the inn.

"Who's up for one last trip through the haunted house?" Leo calls out.

"Fine," I say.

"I'll be right there with you, Bizzy," Jasper says as he lands a kiss to my cheek.

Emmie nods. "And then we can head to the café and eat all the cupcakes we want."

"I'm in," I say.

We hit that haunted house not once but *six* times in keeping with the sinister theme of the night.

We eat our fill of cupcakes, then head out toward the cove where the waves are wild, and the wind is cutting and mean.

The sound of howls lights up the night as the dogs and Fish run from one end of the cove to the other.

And in the distance, in the woods just past the café, I spot an entire army of red beady eyes staring this way, and along with them are giggling women all too eager to keep company with the beasts at hand. If I'm not mistaken, I think I see Georgie, Juni, Camila, Macy, and my mother.

"True to Gentry's word, it looks as if the werewolves showed up after all," I say, pulling Jasper close. "I think a wild time will be had by all."

"Let's head back to the cottage," he says, nipping at my neck. "I think we've got a wild night ahead of us, too."

"Why, Detective, it's as if you've read my mind."

We say goodnight to Emmie and Leo and head back home, where a howling good time is had well into the night.

The holidays are coming, and Cider Cove is about to be

transformed into the holy town of Bethlehem just in time for Christmas. Here's hoping nothing unholy happens in the month of December.

The inn will be hosting a wedding—one that I cannot wait to be a part of.

Here's hoping the inn doesn't live up to its haunted reputation.

A shiver runs through me at the thought.

Something tells me it's going to be a miracle if we all come out of the holidays alive.

And something tells me one of us won't.

RECIPE

Spider Web Cupcakes
Country Cottage Café

Hello, it's me, Bizzy! Halloween has descended on ~~Cider~~ Spider Cove and things have been pretty Spooktacular around here—with the exception of that dead body, of course. But homicides aside, Emmie has managed to make this haunted holiday a culinary delight with her delicious Spider Web Cupcakes. You'll want to whip up a dozen or two or *three* to delight all of the little ghouls in your life. And don't forget to keep a few, or a lot, for yourself!

Happy haunted baking!

Ingredients

1 cup sifted all-purpose flour
¾ cup unsweetened natural baking cocoa
½ cup granulated sugar
½ cup brown sugar

2 eggs (room temperature)
¼ tsp salt
1 tsp baking powder
½ tsp baking soda
1/3 cup vegetable oil
½ cup buttermilk
2 tablespoon vanilla extract

Directions

Preheat oven 350°

Line a 12 cup muffin pan with cupcake liners (*Emmie says purple, orange, green, or silver are fun colors to work with!)

In a large bowl whisk together flour, cocoa powder, baking powder, baking soda, and salt.

In a medium bowl whisk together eggs, granulated sugar, brown sugar, vegetable oil, and vanilla.

Mix wet ingredients into dry ingredients, slowly pouring buttermilk as you combine the two. Don't over stir the batter.

Ladle into cupcake liners, filling each one halfway.

Bake for 15-20 minutes until a toothpick comes out clean.

Vanilla Buttercream Frosting

Ingredients

1 cup unsalted butter (room temperature)
4-5 cups powdered sugar

¼ cup heavy cream
2 teaspoons vanilla extract
A pinch of salt

Directions

*Emmie prefers to use her stand mixer with the paddle attachment for this, but a handheld mixer works well, too.

Beat butter until smooth and creamy for about two minutes. Add four cups of powdered sugar, heavy cream, vanilla extract, and pinch of salt. Beat on high for about two minutes. If the consistency is too thin add more powdered sugar until desired consistency is achieved.

Scoop out approximately ¼ of the frosting and add either purple or black food coloring to create the web pattern.

Frost cupcakes with a half inch of frosting, creating a smooth surface.

Add the colored frosting to a small piping bag. (Emmie likes to put it into a plastic sandwich bag and cuts a very small hole at the tip. This is her go-to piping bag for all simple decorating!)

To create the spider web patten, start by creating a tight spiral from the center of the cupcake and work your way out all the way to the edge. Then, with either a toothpick, or a butterknife, gently score the spiral into four equal parts, starting from the center of the spiral working your way out to the edge in a straight line.

Share with *fiends*, family, boys, and ghouls. Even the most ornery monster is sure to love these.

Enjoy and happy haunted Halloween!

A NOTE FROM THE AUTHORS

Look for **'Twas the Night Before Murder (Country Cottage Mysteries 21)** coming up next!

Thank you for reading **Happy Howl-o-ween Horror (Country Cottage Mysteries 20).** If you enjoyed this book, please consider leaving a review at your point of purchase. Even a sentence or two makes a difference to an author. Thank you so very much in advance! Your effort is very much appreciated.

BOOKS BY ADDISON MOORE

Paranormal Women's Fiction
Hot Flash Homicides
Midlife in Glimmerspell
Wicked in Glimmerspell
Mistletoe in Glimmerspell

Cruising Through Midlife
Cruising Through Midlife

Cozy Mysteries

Meow for Murder
An Awful Cat-titude
A Dreadful Meow-ment
A Claw-some Affair
A Haunted Hallow-whiskers
A Candy Cane Cat-astrophe
A Purr-fect Storm
A Fur-miliar Fatality

Country Cottage Mysteries
Kittyzen's Arrest
Dog Days of Murder
Santa Claws Calamity

Bow Wow Big House

Murder Bites

Felines and Fatalities

A Killer Tail

Cat Scratch Cleaver

Just Buried

Butchered After Bark

A Frightening Fangs-giving

A Christmas to Dismember

Sealed with a Hiss

A Winter Tail of Woe

Lock, Stock, and Feral

Itching for Justice

Raining Cats and Killers

Death Takes a Holiday

Copycat Killer Thriller

Happy Howl-o-ween Horror

Twas the Night Before Murder

Country Cottage Boxed Set 1

Brambleberry Bay Murder Club
Brambleberry Bay Murder Club

Murder in the Mix Mysteries

Cutie Pies and Deadly Lies

Bobbing for Bodies

Pumpkin Spice Sacrifice

Gingerbread & Deadly Dread

Seven-Layer Slayer

Red Velvet Vengeance

Bloodbaths and Banana Cake

New York Cheesecake Chaos

Lethal Lemon Bars

Macaron Massacre

Wedding Cake Carnage

Donut Disaster

Toxic Apple Turnovers

Killer Cupcakes

Pumpkin Pie Parting

Yule Log Eulogy

Pancake Panic

Sugar Cookie Slaughter

Devil's Food Cake Doom

Snickerdoodle Secrets

Strawberry Shortcake Sins

Cake Pop Casualties

Flag Cake Felonies

Peach Cobbler Confessions

Poison Apple Crisp

Spooky Spice Cake Curse

Pecan Pie Predicament

Eggnog Trifle Trouble

Waffles at the Wake

Raspberry Tart Terror

Baby Bundt Cake Confusion

Chocolate Chip Cookie Conundrum

Wicked Whoopie Pies

Key Lime Pie Perjury

Red, White, and Blueberry Muffin Murder

Honey Buns Homicide

Apple Fritter Fright

Vampire Brownie Bite Bereavement

Pumpkin Roll Reckoning

Cookie Exchange Execution

Christmas Fudge Fatality

Murder in the Mix Boxed Sets
Murder in the Mix (Books 1-3)

Mystery
Little Girl Lost
Never Say Sorry
The First Wife's Secret

Head over to Addisonmoore.com for complete list of novels.

ACKNOWLEDGMENTS

Thank YOU, the reader, for joining us on this adventure to Cider Cove. We hope you're enjoying the Country Cottage Mysteries as much as we are. Don't miss **Twas the Night Before Murder** coming up next. It's Christmas in Cider Cove!

Thank you so much from the bottom of our hearts for taking this journey with us. We cannot wait to take you back to Cider Cove!

Special thank you to the following people for taking care of this book—Kaila Eileen Turingan-Ramos, Jodie Tarleton, Margaret Lapointe, Amy Barber, and Lisa Markson. And a very big shout out to Lou Harper of Cover Affairs for designing the world's best covers.

A heartfelt thank you to Paige Maroney Smith for being so amazing in every single way.

And last, but never least, thank you to Him who sits on the throne. Worthy is the Lamb! Glory and honor and power are yours. We owe you everything, Jesus.

ABOUT THE AUTHORS

Addison Moore is a **New York Times, USA TODAY,** and **Wall Street Journal** bestselling author. Her work has been featured in **Cosmopolitan** Magazine. Previously she worked as a therapist on a locked psychiatric unit for nearly a decade. She resides on the West Coast with her husband, four wonderful children, and two dogs where she eats too much chocolate and stays up way too late. When she's not writing, she's reading. Addison's Celestra Series has been optioned for film by **20th Century Fox.**

Bellamy Bloom is a **USA TODAY** bestselling author who writes cozy mysteries filled with humor, intrigue and a touch of the supernatural. When she's not writing up a murderous storm she's snuggled by the fire with her two precious pooches, chewing down her to-be-read pile and drinking copious amounts of coffee.